L U C I F E R :

Soldiers, Serpents, and Sin

Interlude 1:

TOO MANY WINGS

David M. Taylor II

HODT BOOKS, INC.

GURNEE, IL 60031

Lucifer: Soldiers, Serpents and Sin Too Many Wings Interlude 1
1st Edition, Softcover – Published in 2022 by
HOUSE OF DT BOOKS
PO Box 67
Gurnee, IL 60031.
ISBN: 979-8-9871368-0-5
Library of Congress Control Number: 2022919499

Publisher's Cataloging-in-Publication Data
Names: Taylor, David M., II.
Title: Lucifer soldiers, serpents and sin : too many wings interlude 1 / David M. Taylor II.
Description: Skokie, IL : House of DT Books, 2022. | Includes 1 color map. | Summary: A fictional exploration of the War in Heaven between Lucifer and Michael before Earth was created, right after Lucifer launches his first wave of Rebellion, and all of the fallout that accompanies the fact that Lucifer rebelled in the first place.
Identifiers: LCCN 2022919499 | ISBN 9798987136805 (pbk.) | ISBN 9798987136812 (ebook)
Subjects: LCSH: Angels – Fiction. | Bible. Genesis – Fiction. | Heaven – Fiction. | Devil – Fiction. | BISAC: FICTION / Christian / Biblical. | FICTION / Christian / Fantasy. | FICTION / Religious.
Classification: LCC PS3620.A95 L83 2022 | DDC 813 T39--dc23 LC record available at https://lccn.loc.gov/2022919499

For permission or requests, write to the Publisher:
HOUSE OF DT BOOKS
PO Box 67
Gurnee, IL 60031.
House.of.dt@gmail.com

Printed in the USA
10 9 8 7 6 5 4 3 2 1

TABLE OF CONTENTS
Mensam de Content

OTHER CONTENT IN THE REALM SERIES
Alius Contentus

4,000 YEARS BEFORE LUCIFER
The Order of Orali.
Graphic Novel
Coming Soon

3,000 YEARS BEFORE LUCIFER
The Curse of Jophiel.
Graphic Novel
Coming Soon

ONE YEAR BEFORE EARTH – LUCIFER'S REBELLION
Lucifer: Soldiers, Serpents and Sin – A Clash of Lightning and Thunder. Book 1.
Novel
Available Now on Amazon: https://amzn.to/3T6NApA

Animals of The Realm
Coloring Book
Available Now on Amazon: https://amzn.to/3rUnOIS

FOUR DAYS AFTER THE REBELLION
Lucifer: Soldiers, Serpents and Sin – Too Many Wings Interlude 1.
Novella
Available Now on Amazon

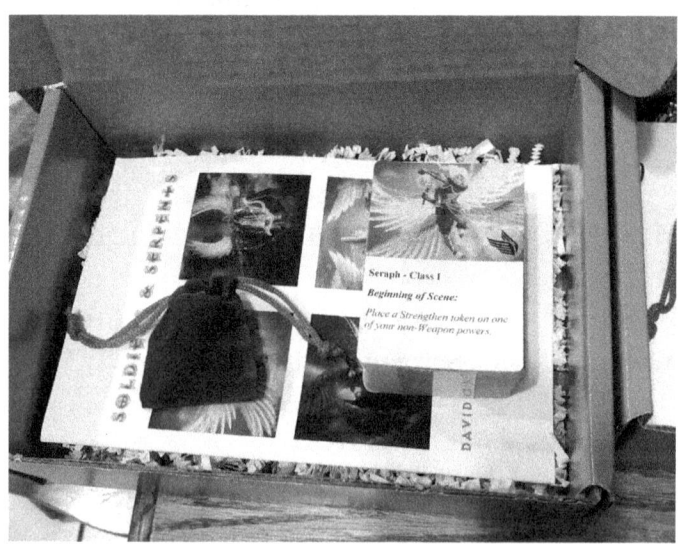

NINE MONTHS AFTER THE REBELLION
Lucifer: Soldiers, Serpents and Sin –
The Tongue that Shook the World
Book 4
Novel
Coming Soon

5,000 YEARS AFTER THE REBELLION
Flight of the Alembi
Story Book
Coming Soon

The Nephilim Wars
Comic Book Series
Available Now through www.NucleusComics.com

DEDICATION
Dedication

This book is dedicated to lovers of Fantasy, lovers of Truth,
those that can see beyond the Veil,
and those that want a leg up in the fight.

Always easier to win when you know how your opponent thinks.

PREFACE
Praefatio

As I say in every piece of content in this series, you have to read/consume it all to get the whole story.

On the page Other Content in the Realm Series, you can see what else is happening in the story world, as it is quite vast.

Your experience will only be enriched every time you pick up a new piece of content.

NOTE FROM THE AUTHOR
Nota ex Auctore

Thank you so much for taking time out of your life to read one of my books. I too have gone to school, parented, worked two to three jobs, and chased my dream, all at the same time.

So I know how precious time spent is.

Becoming an author for me was a matter of coming back to one of my first loves. I've been writing since I was very young, but along with my songwriting, I did not take it seriously at first. I did not see myself doing it for a living. And then I started collecting comic books.

My father taught me to read using comics, and I knew that I wanted to be one of those people that created the stories. It took me a long time to get from being that lad that loved to read and write to publishing my first full novel. Many years of chasing the wrong dream.

What turned it around for me was taking what had been an idea/vision of the first time the devil saw his reflection in the waters of Eden and just plain running with it.

I literally just sat down one day and started writing and let my imagination explode.

What happened when Lucifer realized that he'd become a monster? I wondered what that must have been like. Because that exact same process can happen to us as people,

and I wanted to study it to learn how all of humanity could avoid sharing in that particularly horrific fate.

It went from a ten-page story to this whole series. It took, and is taking, a lot of blood, sweat, tears, and many sleepless nights to develop this story world.

And it's been the validation from readers of that first novel becoming a best-seller on Amazon that's kept me going.

It helps me so completely and thoroughly when you write reviews. It helps me with the Amazon algorithm, helps more people become encouraged to explore this series, and hopefully ignites aspiring authors to go ahead and jump out there to make it happen for themselves.

I read each and every one of these book reviews personally, because they mean so much to me. And I can't thank you enough for the time you take to write them.

You have to be signed into your Amazon account to do this, but if you wouldn't mind, please leave me a review for this book by copying and pasting the following links into your browser:

Paperback: http://www.amazon.com/review/create-review?&asin=B0BSJ6HVYX
eBook: https://www.amazon.co.uk/review/create-review?&asin=B0BSSGCCY6

I will pour over and appreciate every single word.

Thank you from the bottom of my heart.

MAP
Directiones

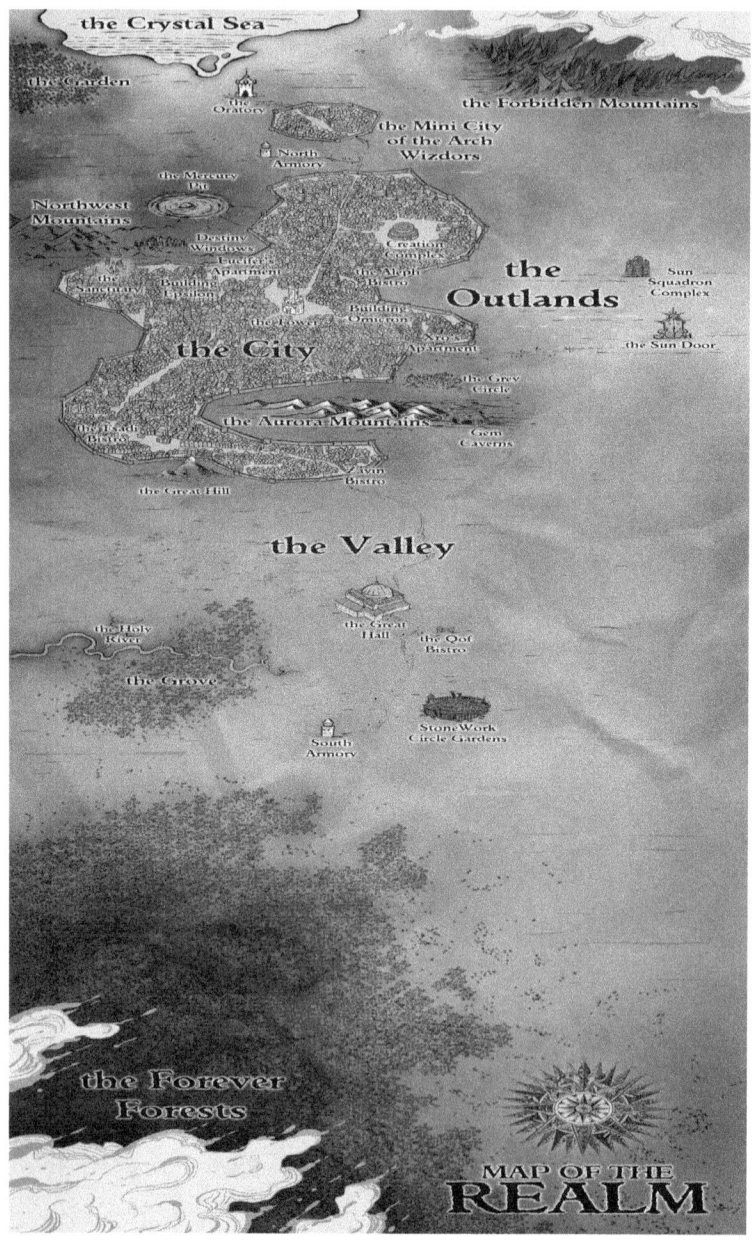

CAST OF CHARACTERS
Mittite ex Personae

ARIEL ARCH WIZDOR – The only female in the entire Realm, she is known for her beauty, her flight speed, her singing voice, and her ability to mesmerize any of the brethren. Only appears every thirty days and is otherwise in the form of Uriel.

AZAZEAL – Originally a two-armed, two-winged Class III Grigori, he wanted to gain the respect of his peers. He purposed to fly behind the Wall of Light to directly gaze upon The Throne and ended up getting badly burned, along with all that followed him. Later adapted the name Xro.

AZAZEALITES – Mutated former Class III Grigori who, due to their attempt to fly behind the Wall of Light, have fused noses and mouths, melted skin, and permanently burnt wings. They can barely breathe, are nearsighted, and their wings are too singed to grant them flight capability.

EREMIEL ARCH WIZDOR – Chief metallurgist, weapons designer and armor maker for The Realm.

ERIS – One of the seven Kroni, and a Class II Cherubim. Member of Lucifer's Loyalist army.

GABRIEL ARCH WIZDOR – One of The Big Three, Gabriel is the multilingual, seven-winged Messenger for all The Realm. He commands his army of Messengers to deliver information as well.

I O A N – One of the seven Kroni, and a Class II Cherubim. Worship Leader protégé of Lucifer.

I R I N – One-meter-tall brethren with square faces set in square heads. They possess beady black eyes, are perpetually hungry, and have flight patterns like slow butterflies, since their wings are perpetually dirty and out of joint. Members of Lucifer's Loyalist army.

I T H O D O R – Junior Gladiator, formed in the left side of the cocoon with his twin brother, Ithokor. Possesses the ability to sense death.

I T H O K O R – Junior Gladiator, formed on the right side of the cocoon with his twin brother, Ithodor. Possesses Third Sight, the ability to see the auras and energy that surround and inhabit the brethren.

K R E E R – One of the seven Kroni, and a Class II Cherubim. Member of Lucifer's Loyalist army.

K R O N I – A Cherubim class of brethren that can write their own music and liturgy for worship in Gathering. Lucifer was the first, and there were seven others besides him.

L O Y A L I S T A R M Y – Lucifer's troops that he rallied to his side to create the Rebellion, and usher in the New Order. The army was made up of at least one member of every class of brethren, with some classes numbering into the tens of millions.

L U C I F E R – Four-winged anointed Class II Cherubim, owner of the Coat of Many Gems, the first Kroni, Worship Leader, Composer, possessor of an internal Pipe Organ and Tabrets, Light Bearer, the Morningson, Prince of the Grigori, Founder and Leader of the Rebellion.

MICHAEL ARCH WIZDOR – One of the Chief Princes of the brethren, and one of The Big Three, known for his massive emerald wings and enormous strength. Head of the Gladiator class and Minister of Defense for The Realm.

NODOX – One of the seven Kroni, and a Class II Cherubim. Member of Lucifer's Loyalist army.

PEREPHAN – One of the seven Kroni, and a Class II Cherubim. Member of Lucifer's Loyalist army.

RÁFOS – One of the seven Kroni, and a Class II Cherubim. Member of Lucifer's Loyalist army.

RAPHAEL ARCH WIZDOR – Chief Healer and leader of the Healer brethren. Raphael is also Keeper of The Leaves.

RZIE – General of the Azazealite army under Uza's leadership.

TRISTAN – One of the seven Kroni, and a Class II Cherubim. Member of Lucifer's Loyalist army.

URIEL ARCH WIZDOR – One of The Big Three, known for his infectious laugh and powerful singing voice, he is the Chief Negotiator and Mediator for The Realm. He is the only one of The Big Three to not command an army. Transforms every thirty days into Ariel.

UZA – Leader of the Azazealites, succeeding Xro.

XRO – Originally known as Azazeal, and right-hand assistant to Lucifer. He had a harness specially created for him by Lucifer to help him fly.

ZERMES – The copper-skinned, black-winged flight trainer for all the brethren, and the last known member of the Dominion class.

Written in the Scrolls.Martyría Pápyros ton matión
Pre-Earth 00-XVI-VIDCC
Gestianolous Cycle 93.050
Ektós chrónou
Éxo apó tous kýlindroi

PROLOGUE 1
Praefatio Ūnus

The mind says it's impossible. Experience says it's risky.Ç
Reason says it doesn't make any sense.
The heart says try it anyway.

~Orali the Great

FOUR DAYS AFTER THE REBELLION

2:13 PRIMORDIAL

The Mole

Even in a singsong way, he couldn't find the words. He knew they were there on the tip of his tongue because he felt them dancing in his saliva. But they wouldn't form and come out.

He wiped a glob of sweat out of his left eye and looked up. *Pushing is probably my best bet at this point*, he assessed. *And by 'best' I mean 'only.'* His bunched-up muscles strained as he surreptitiously pushed to his left. Sinewy shoulders knotting, runny nose snotting, and pencil-thin trickles of sweat scurrying down his throbbing back, he dug in deeper. His heaving lungs were petitioning for secession from his chest, and the stale brown air wasn't helping.

He ignored its rancidness, stopping for a moment to step back. In any other context, he would've considered that laziness. But his subconscious knew the horrible truth: the wall was symbolic.

Comeuppance solidified. An emblematic memento of the past, staring him right in the face, judging him about everything that had led him here.

So granting himself only the briefest moment of respite, he inhaled sharply and leaned in again as hard as he could. His feet etched their mark in the dust like a bizarre ground tattoo, his knees nearly buckling as they supported his odd frame. He grunted and pushed like his life depended on it.

And nothing moved.

I'm not getting anywhere with this, the Mole thought. *And those aren't thoughts I'm used to thinking.*

Tired eyes narrowed as he more fully surveyed the terrain, his thoughts racing out ahead of his gaze. Things had changed, and quite quickly. His mind spit out the raw truth of his ugly dilemma, facing the obvious.

At first there was little chance of connecting with Michael without Lucifer knowing. So with precision that rivaled a thousand Oralian sharpswords, he'd managed to contact the leader of the Arch Wizdors in the most clandestine of ways.

But now...now there may be no way to contact Michael at all. Pictures of the good old days began to flicker through his head, but he shut them down. Grimacing, he turned his focus upward, moving his head in a semi-circle, counting everything around him. Numbering things tended to help quiet his conflicted cranium. Smoother breaths started to flow, with no sound accompanying them. Meditation always helped him metaphorically peer over enough ledges to know which one held the answer.

Then the words came.

And they weren't problem solving words at all. They were, however, strangely and satisfyingly...pungent.

Prologue 1

Curse Michael, he thought, snarling. *Curse him and everybody that looks like him.*

PROLOGUE 2
Praefatio Duo

The Dimensioners froze and collectively held their breath for a beat…and then the front ten rows screamed with an unfamiliar battle cry, lunging through the smoke at the Throneists and their bleeding captain. They fought like furious pit bulls, going for their throats with little to no concern for their own lives. As the clang and rattle of the hostile melee filled the air, Tull raised his shield and flew closer to Captain L'sinell.

"This fighting sir…it doesn't make any sense."

"Tell me about it, Tull," said L'sinell, dodging another arrow. "We're supposed to be cleaning up, not still fighting. Especially with those recruited to be our *allies*. We absolutely cannot afford to lose any more food stores."

Tull followed L'sinell's line of sight only to observe an even more worrying scene.

Not all of the Dimensioners were engaged in combat. Many of them continued snarfing food, filling their empty pouches and their various esophagi with it, stopping only to fight when a Throneist engaged them.

Tull swung his shield sharply across his body, stopping three thunderspears in midair amidst looking at what he saw in their ration packs.

"You're right, Captain. We most certainly can't."

"I've never seen anything like this." L'sinell grimaced as a fresh forearm cut started bleeding. "This situation is out of control. It needs to be contained and neutralized immediately. Because it's going to draw the worst possible kind of attention."

"And," continued L'sinell, "I don't even want to *think* about what would happen if Raphael Arch Wizdor were to show up here."

CRYSTAL FACES

Capitulum Nihil

11:44 PRIMORDIAL

Southeast Rooms
Level 3
The South Armory

"There is no time for ye olde stupid questions!", the voice emerged from one of the armored figures, as they traded blows in quick succession.

"I *said*…where is the training?" the other one replied with a quick response, triggering the first into a natural, almost gracile defense stance

"Have at thee then, ye brutish lout!" replied, again, the first figure with another quick strike. The two were exchanging words as their unearthly swords clashed with each other in a beautiful, yet dangerous dance.

"I say thee nay, thou foul contender!"

The second figure let his sword slide slightly, edge to edge, with his opponent facing him in an offensive glare. The two swords, made of fire and lightning, made a surprisingly beautiful sound as they moved slowly from each other. Suddenly, the clash came again, as the first contending figure attacked fiercely. "Thou shalt not vanquish me with yon lightning, thou broccoli-breath'd worm!" yelled the first figure with a note of irony in his silky voice.

The swords came into quick succession, encountering their pair in each strike, as the second warrior answered "my lightning is more than enough for you, thou king of morons and chicken!" in a tense, yet juvenile voice.

The swords seemed, at this point, dancing a song on their own, clashing and bashing with each other, shedding beautiful yet terrifying sounds each time they touched each other. Without any sign of change, all of the sudden, there was a whooshing sound, instantly changing the cadence of the sparring song.

Ithodor blinked when he realized that in the middle of their blazing fast sparring, he'd missed his brother completely. Without sound, he took off his heavy helmet and shut down his sizzling lightning sword, jostling his wings to land one step away from his twin. He stared like they'd just met.

Intricately carved statues lined the roof of the South Armory, almost like silent sentinels keeping watch over the brothers. Said statues also covered every corner and filled every internal room, both in the ceiling and on the floor. The arena the twins occupied was a perfect square comprised of marble, wood, glass, stone and brick, and it was full of those exquisite works of art.

The delicate sculptures were there as memorials, carved out to commemorate brethren that had distinguished themselves in the service of The Throne. The Armory's outer rim was also covered with golden-copper likenesses of some of the Realm's most notable brethren. Ithokor thought all of that to be the height of irony, given their present reality.

Swiftly standing back upright after avoiding his brother's blow, his loose gold armor jangling like old chains, Ithokor attempted to hide the cavalcade of chuckles he felt bubbling up from his stomachs.

"So I'm the Moron Chicken King, huh? Yeah and verily, you couldn't hit a tree if you were close enough to eat its bark."

"How…how did you…?"

Ithokor rolled his still glistening eyes. "They keep saying we're the same age Dor, but the Creation Cocoons really must have favored me in the parturition and spit me out first. Along with a full supply of brains. And you, you got… well, I don't exactly know what it is you've got. Besides being formed in the left Cocoon with a face that looks like day-old pizza. Selah."

"You shouldn't…you shouldn't have been able to avoid that strike, Kor…"

"And yet? Here we are."

"As much as I enjoy speakin' formally even when those snobbish Seraphim aren't around…you do realize that you also parried my question, right?"

"Your brain power is uncanny."

"Uh huh. A question I will now repeat: where is our training?"

"Well, we're here, Dor. And the lightning swords are flying. And missing. Score another DUHR prize for Mr. 'Second Sight.'"

"Yeah thanks a bushel for bringing *that* up."

"Yeah well, I've got Third Sight."

Ithodor raised one eyebrow.

"So….you're accepting it now? And that's what you're calling it?"

"Not in front of polite company, Captain Death Siren. As opposed to, you know….the walking media exposé known as my twin."

"So instead, I should suck up to those snooty Seraphim like you do? And for the record, that Second Sight you keep trying to shush out of me almost–"

"Almost what? Got us killed? Embarrassed me down to the last feather on my wings?"

Ithodor held his head down. "But Kor… we… we won," he said pensively. "The Throneists won. And we helped save the day. Didn't we?"

"*Did* we?"

Ithodor found himself suddenly wordless. The normally loquacious twin smelled the musk and sweat in the South Armory's rear training room surrounding them, and it felt heavier than usual. Folding their wings down into resting position, with the pine green feathers snugly nestling into the centers of their respective backs, the events of the last week hung between the siblings like soot in the air.

Ithokor broke the awkward silence.

"That's your problem, spaghetti lips."

"What's my 'problem,' Kor? And for the record my lips are *not*–"

"You presume too much, brother. That's what makes you telegraph your finishing move. And I mean, every single time, Selah. You keep believing that speed is enough. That's incorrect. Maybe we can ask Michael to glue a spatial geometry calculator to your face–"

"Are we talking about our sparring sessions, Kor? Or everything that happened this week and all the gushing purple bruises we have to show for it? I can barely sleep now, did you know that?"

"Of course I know that–"

"And when I can't sleep, I can't think. Closing my eyes makes me see…things that I wish I hadn't seen. All those brethren, our own friends, melted together in a pile of slag," said Ithodor.

"I see Lucifer's overpowered form," said Ithokor. "He was a dragon and his shape got contorted until his very body angles were not possible…just not possible," his voice trailing off.

Ithodor kicked his booted toe on the ground.

"I *did* sense Death, y'know… and I was right. Are we just ignoring that too?"

"…We are not ignoring anything, brother."

"And by 'anything' you mean—oh, I dunno—like the fact that we got sent out here and haven't heard from Uriel in four days?"

Another interminable beat of silence went on.

"I'm sure… I'm sure he has his reasons," said a suddenly uncertain sounding Ithokor.

"And as ALWAYS you defend him. What IS it with you?"

"Nothing is 'with' me you caramel twit. I got the brain between us, remember?"

"Sure you did. Let me count the lobes. I'm the odd brother out, as ALWAYS, evidenced by the fact that we've been holed up in here, by ourselves, for the last four days. Just the two of us, training while waiting to train so we can train for our training. 'Wait until you get a load of Earth,' he said."

Ithokor scowled as Ithodor mocked Uriel's hearty voice.

"'You're going to get your next-level gladiator training,'" Ithodor scorned.

"I will repeat: He. Has. His. Reasons. And," continued Ithokor, "a little solitude is sometimes a good thing. A necessary thing."

"Uh huh," said Ithodor. "A *lifetime* of solitude however–"

"LOOK BRO. We did graduate to the next gladiator level. Just like Uriel promised. And you *will* show some respect." Ithokor sighed and shook his head. "I swear…that unbridled mouth of yours–"

"Is just like yours, Kor. Except according to you, with more spaghetti."

Ithokor frowned again. "That's not even–"

The floor of the Armory suddenly trembled. Several unpolished plaques violently fell off of the east wall, fracturing into splinters as they struck the ground. Behind them, three windows stress shattered, and the unmistakable scent of burning flesh wafted into the room.

Without hesitation Ithodor unfurled his corpulent wings and flew in a beeline towards the nearest intact Armory window.

"Wait, Dor! WAIT! Crump it all, we don't even know what that is–"

"All the more reason to look and see. Bruh."

Ithokor swiftly caught up to his brother as Ithodor was pressing his face against the dull yellow pane. His twin followed suit as his eyes stretched saucer wide.

Lucifer's Loyalist Cherubim–who had been hiding in the northeast corner as an auriferous statue–turned two of the eyes in his lower wings to the right. He was trying not to flinch so the twins wouldn't notice him since he wanted to see, too.

With an identical expression etched on the skin of both their faces, the gladiators-in-training found themselves staring out of the ornamented window feeling one thing–shock.

"Um…are you sure it isn't time for a ye olde stupid question?" asked Ithodor.

There had been an explosion. A huge one. In The Grove.

Right where most of the remaining food stores were.

Chapter 1

LEAPS AND BOUNDARIES
Capitulum Ūnus

11:57 PRIMORDIAL

The Outskirts of Proxima Centauri

"Put that silver DOWN!"

"And break left! *NOW!*"

In a corner of space that was four and one quarter light years from Sol, the sun-bronzed gladiator known as G'zrem didn't hesitate, even though dust particles were whipping past his blinking eyes. Michael, the unquestioned Chief of Gladiators, had crisply, in baritone, spoken an order. So even with thoughts of murder—being on the receiving end of it from a Luciferian, not committing it himself—still racing through his head, G'zrem banked left. The mid-sized gladiator put his silver away and grasped his crackling lightning sword by its ornamented hilt, holding it parallel to his perfectly-arched-for-flying body. He steadied the weapon in his tense grip, its pulsating blade only scant millimeters from his nose.

He held his gaze level as the careening asteroids pelted the air around him. His blazing sword split the larger chunked debris in two right in front of him as he cut a tenuous swath through the hurtling horde of rocks.

There shouldn't be wind shear in space, G'zrem thought, but the smell of burning paper seemed to accompany the all-encompassing rock storm. *And Michael is watching*, knots forming in his stomach as his lips stretched into a thin line.

The nearest green-winged gladiator to his right, his friend Atiel, was busy decimating flying detritus at top speed as well, but their tired shoulders and splatter-crusted armor told the real story: this asteroid field felt more like a spatial ocean of endless, rusty fragments.

The bizarre scene continued: latent comets surrounding them, pockets of gaseous anomalies enveloping them, mini-stars glittering against the unyielding blackness of space. The celestial elements silently hailed them, watching Michael and his gladiatorial cadre hastening towards Proxima. Growing weary of the sustained–yet unpostponable–activity, G'zrem thought:

We shouldn't even be here again. But the initial cleanup wasn't nearly as complete as I thought.

The unexplained asteroid field continued covering the area surrounding Proxima Centauri as if the star itself had moved into a new galaxial landscape.

Michael scrunched his nose. *Four hours. Four hours of unbroken flying through this swarm of debris at feather singeing speed, trying to clear it... and we haven't made a dent.*

A flash of burnt orange off of the helmet of G'zrem's steady cranium was enough to change Michael's mind. And then it hit him like a slab of uncut palladium:

This isn't an asteroid field. And that means....

"INCOMING!" Michael roared, snapping his head up. "Gladiators! Delta formation! NOW!"

As one, with a precision that defied description, the forty gladiators on Michael's left, in perfect unison with the forty on his right extended their respective right wings. They then stretched out their right arms with it....and with a sudden *SNAP* they closed ranks tightly with only millimeters between them. Michael's silver eyes could see their thoughts running through the nerves of their tensed lips, as they wondered why such a dangerous formation of speed was called for. Their ignited lighting swords alone, if cross streamed, could cause an electrical discharge that would blow them all out of space.

That was the precise moment that fourteen unmanned copper warp spheres materialized from multiple vectors around them, careening towards them at forty-five-degree angles from their origin point.

"Put down your faceplates and shut your eyes!" barked Michael.

".....What?" whispered one of the Gladiators.

"I said FACEPLATES DOWN AND EYES SHUT, SOLDIER! SHUT THEM *NOW!*"

Without warning, Proxima Centauri's brightness increased tenfold. The resulting flare would've temporarily blinded Michael's gladiators had they not clamped down tightly and shielded their eyes. The copper warp sphere navigation systems scrambled with the sudden surge of magnetic activity from the star, and they started colliding with the gladiators from all directions. Except they were moving at ten times the speed they'd first had when they materialized. It sounded like boulders thudding against concrete walls as the gladiators stoically clenched their jaws against the sudden pelting. Michael had at least three copper warp spheres hit him squarely on his right shoulder, but he held his ground without so much as a grunt.

Sphere after sphere pounded away at his cabal of warriors as they held formation.

We can't risk detonating them! Michael fought his instinct to raise his lightning sword.

There may be enough explosive charges in them to level this whole star system...

They huddled and grit their teeth. Sweat and bruises accumulated quickly. G'zrem felt like his stomach was crawling up to his mouth. *Too many! Too close!*

After a seemingly interminable lapse of time, the circular containers of death seemed to stop coming, the way a sudden thunderstorm seems to change its mind after venting its rage.

With a buzzing sound, a distinct voice emerged from the immensity of space:

<Michael, this is Gabriel. Michael this is Gabriel, do you copy, over!>

Ignoring his brother's voice, Michael slowly lifted his eyes above the folded shield of his emerald wings. The last of the spheres seemed to be scurrying past them three meters above their heads. His singed wings slowly flaked off one by one. Michael waited another beat and finally exhaled a command.

"Squadron...at ease," said the muscular Chief Gladiator.

As one, his troops began to break formation and look around them. Many had to stifle a gasp as they looked in the distance to see the number of spheres that had just assailed them. It looked to number in the hundreds. The still spiraling spheres looked like buzzing bees on the prowl for something to sting, and some did indeed begin to explode with varying levels of discharge.

"What...what happened, sir?" Atiel asked, still staring at the copper assailants.

The warrior in Michael wanted to count this narrow avoidance of fatal pummeling as a win....just like that same internal warrior voice was trying to do with the events of the last week. But the soldier in Michael knew better. Lucifer had literally been in the details, and it was his preoccupation with his *other* problem that caused him to do a less than thorough job on Proxima a few days ago. That lack of thoroughness was now costing them. The Chief Gladiator then reached a sharp conclusion about a suddenly very deadly reality for him and his cadre.

"We're going to have to do another weapons sweep, gladiators." Michael tried his best to keep the subtle hint of a disappointed sigh out of his tone. *Another sweep of Proxima means that my issue back home is going to become, temporarily, a secondary issue. And it definitely is not secondary.*

Michael saw Atiel and a few others cock their heads to the right; his soldiers would never question him, but that look meant that they didn't quite understand the order either.

Michael inhaled. "That so-called 'asteroid field' was nothing of the kind. Those were actually remnants of copper warp spheres encrusted with dirt. Lucifer left them blanketing the area, operatin' on some kind of magnetic charge. He also programmed the intact ones we just avoided with a type of proximity trigger, so that anyone that dared to brave the swarming shrapnel would be assaulted by fully functional spheres. And all of that," said Michael, "would be exacerbated by the random flares that Proxima Centauri, as a red dwarf star, is known to have, triggered by the increased magnetic activity."

"Will they come back?" asked someone on Michael's left. "And what does all of what you said mean for us now?"

"They may possibly." Michael stretched his aching wings and all forty of his troops followed suit. "Every sensor they have is now probably fried and confused, but there could some type of boomerang mechanism on them. And as I'm unsure as to their payload, we couldn't risk detonation by slicing our swords through them. I'm assuming that the varying levels of magnetic particles between the star, our armor, and their own composition stopped them from all simultaneously exploding, but that is a random element that could not be accounted for. Or duplicated."

Michael turned his head to look several meters in front of them. "In terms of what that means for us now…"

His brother's voice interrupted him again.

<Michael, come in. Answer me. This is Gabriel. Michael this is Gabriel, do you copy, over.>

"We didn't even have time to bring our lightning swords to bear for that second round," said Atiel. "We might've been crushed and then dismembered by those teleporting spheres if…if not for your leadership, sir. Thank you," he said, as the rest of the gladiators began to nod.

"No need for thanks," said Michael. "Obedience saves lives. Write *that* in gold."

Michael's shimmering silver eyes narrowed, sweeping his gaze back and forth around their current position. He knew now to constantly check for any further covert surprises that Lucifer may have left, as the depths of his former friend's planning was still being discovered. The overt operations of Lucifer were now going to take even more analysis to understand and decrypt. Michael wouldn't comment on what the eyes of his soul now perceived everywhere he turned.

Doing my job means taking calculated risks. But maybe I didn't do all of the calculations, he ruminated to himself.

"Left phalanx," said Michael, "continue in one-quarter delta formation mode, and stay in orbit up here. Alert me immediately if there is any unusual activity, especially if it's anything like what we just saw. Adjust your wrist comms to detect increased magnetic surges. If you see a surge, you have less then point five seconds to shut your eyes and turn away from Proxima, because it's going to flare, and we don't need any damaged retinas out here."

G'zrem smiled as he nodded in the affirmative, as he realized that Michael kept his eyes open even during the peak of the flare. Those silver eyes of his, after being so close to the heat of glory behind The Veil, wouldn't be phased by a temperamental star.

G'zrem also smiled as he reached back into his tunic and found his silver. He tore off the wrapping and took a huge, sloppy bite. Atiel just stared at him.

"What?" asked G'zrem. "Silver-wrapped chocolate. S'best in the Realm. Gladiator perk 'cause I got it special from the chefs at the Tszadi Bistro. Y'know. For energy." G'zrem stuffed his jaws with another chocolate chunk and looked back at a glaring Michael.

"…What?"

"Uh huh. Energy." *You're gonna need it, soldier.*

Michael's tone shifted. "Right phalanx…put down the faceplates of your helmets again and adjust your lenses. Filter out as much light in each spectrum as you can and follow me down closer to Proxima's surface. We can't afford to miss any weapons or booby traps this time, lest some other brethren come through here at some point and suffer a worse fate."

"Sir yes sir!" they said as one. They snapped their helmets and faceplates into position and stood at the ready.

Gabriel's voice pierced the air with an insistency that Michael recognized.

<Michael, Et tu ferais mieux de m'entendre, by the halcyon days of old you are going to wish you had picked up. Don't say I didn't warn you about–>

Michael clicked his commlink and turned his back to his soldiers. G'zrem was busy wiping the chocolate smears off the inside of his faceplate as Atiel rolled his eyes.

"Gabriel, what is it? I don't want to hear anything that doesn't sound like 'we found Eremiel.'"

<Then disappointment will aBOUND but look who realized he was an actual Arch Wizdor and decided to finally answer his comm. GOOD THING it wasn't an emergency or anything grandiose like that and even common *brethren would still have the courtesy to respond. And precisely WHY in the Missing Moons of Mercury are you not back home? Do you HONESTLY know what is happening right now.>*

"Gabriel. Whine less. Communicate more. And slow down."

<Don't tell me to slow down, mein bruder. This is not the time for slowing down.>

"Yeah well, sometimes slowing down and getting it right is the thing that makes the difference. We may have just survived because Lucifer used C4 instead of nitroglycerin. So since my soldiers are waiting for me, I need to–"

<What you need to do is listen.>

With his polylingual tongue engaged, Gabriel quickly explained the reason behind his fast tone and the hurry behind the call. Michael could not believe his increasingly silvering ears, and his tunic felt like it was shrinking around his throat.

"They've done *what?*"

<You heard me.> Gabriel's voice never sounded tired, but sometimes his attitude did.

<They allegedly started fighting over the food stores in the Grove and now there's been an explosion. Said fighting being caused by those brethren you brought in from those other dimensions. The same ones that helped us fight Lucifer.>

And there it is, thought Michael. *My other problem.* The burly Arch Wizdor again mentally chided himself for hoping nothing like this would happen before he got those extra-dimensional brethren back to their proper homes.

He also knew that hope was not a strategy.

"Can't you handle this, Gabriel? I've got to–"

<Raphael is closer than I am. And I am not leaving my Messengers. Plus, I'm still getting full intel on the details. Và có rất nhiều chi tiết. These other dimensional ruffians seem to be, rather voraciously I might add, wolfing down food that doesn't belong to them. And handling it? Is not the issue, Michael. It's that you wouldn't like my solution.>

The canvases of both their minds played out possible Gabriel-led scenarios for a full beat.

<Több van, Michael. There's something you're not telling me. Because I know you. So…what is it?> Gabriel pressed.

"Gabe, look, I–"

<Tick tock, my brother. My Messengers already have too much to deal with as it is. We are backlogged.>

Michael noted Gabriel's signature way of enunciating words that he was incensed by.

<There are major locations that are still in shambles, the Great Hall being one of them. Og vi har ikke råd til problemer i Grove. We are not going to do the job of your gladiators. So a decision needs to be made here, before this situation gets any further out of hand. A situation which–as far as I'm concerned–was never in hand to begin with.>

'In hand,' Michael thought. *Lucifer. You have no idea what you've caused.*

Their commlinks worked Realm-wide but every time Gabriel spoke, Michael's wrist felt like his comm was spitting guilty static. The warrior in him was satisfied with blaming Lucifer, with being glad that at least his former best friend was rotting in Tartarus.

The soldier in him knew it wasn't that simple. And never would be again.

Michael felt the seconds passing like flaming hail. Before last week he would've chuckled at his inegalitarian brother's intuitive sense about him. *But these days…laughter feels like a cheat code.*

The Chief Gladiator inhaled–silently thanking the Throne that they had not lost their ability to breathe in space–then dropped his voice to a level so low that Gabriel was the only living thing in the Realm that could hear him.

"What I haven't told you, Gabriel, is that some of those extra brethren have actually gone over my head. Some of those Dimensioners have in fact started a petition to The Throne to stay in this dimension permanently. They even want to take up residence in The City."

> *<Nuk e besoj!*
> *Cha chreid mi e!*
> *나는 그것을 믿지 않는다!>*

Seventeen different translations of "I don't believe it" spewed out of Michael's comm in less than four seconds. He stopped listening after the third one.

<'Dimensioners' huh?> Gabriel continued. *<That's what you're calling them? Who exactly do they think they are? And what are you going to do about them?>*

"I don't think they all support that petition, Gabe, so the answer to 'who' is multiple choice. *How* they're behaving is what we're dealing with now, and that answer is, 'decidedly unruly.'"

Which I knew, Michael thought, *before I brought them here.*

<Your exponentially naïve outlook on the geometry of the soul notwithstanding, there's a brewing situation in the Grove food stores. That's not tomorrow, that's not after brunch, that's right now. I shouldn't have to remind you how much of those stores your best friend already burned. We are running out of time if containment is your plan. Do you indeed copy that, Michael?>

Michael's face scrunched into a mask of pain as he remembered discovering Kerubiel's corpse not too far from where his gladiators were now. His piercing gaze fell upon his left phalanx flying in orbit over Proxima as he'd ordered them to. He then peered right to see the waiting stares of his right phalanx, poised to fly down to Proxima's surface with him.

The Chief Gladiator knew If he left his troops alone here, there might be some more Luciferian traps that were as yet unsprung. And without his silver eyes and strength, his gladiators could be greatly injured by them, or possibly not survive them at all. His sweat drenched biceps bunched up as his hands curled into a powerful ball.

The upper pockets of space were normally odorless and often deafening in their silence, yet he imagined the clash of lightning and steel that was happening in the Grove right now. His teeth tasted the grit, his nose flared over the bitter scent of smoke and the blackened, bleeding flesh. His lungs also were too familiar with those flavors. Flavors he was responsible for.

The fact remains… those same additional soldiers–and truthfully that's bein' generous–are wreaking havoc. Because they're not supposed to permanently reside in this dimension, whether they understand that or not.

Then there's that whole yet-as-unresolved edict about moving Eden.

Michael came to himself and realized he hadn't answered his brother, but the seven-winged Gabriel was already gone. The ready-to-proceed stares and uniformed flapping wings of his troops weighed a metric ton in his brain, as his own abundantly decorated pine-green wings held him aloft.

He had to make a choice.

And without further hesitation, Michael did.

Chapter 2

SMELLS LIKE ANAMNESIS
Capitulum Duo

12:16 CELESTIAL

Southeast Rooms
Level 3
The South Armory

"I think we should go over there," Ithodor said. "We *have* to go over there."

Turn around, he heard inside his head.

His rapidly numbing cheeks felt like they were being stung by a thousand pins. Ithodor was pressing his face even more tightly against the window.

Turn around. Ithodor heard it again.

No event, not even a sub-lethal explosion, was a match for his brain tingling with inquisitiveness. He peered over his right shoulder, ignoring the dense billowing smoke in front of him, looking intently around the humid training room behind him.

And he saw nothing.

Ithokor didn't move. He just stared as the hypnotic dance of the rising fire twisted and writhed before him, the growing flames morphing from yellow to orange. He didn't know if he was imagining the window itself beginning to turn warm.

"We're not going out there even if we get a gold-encrusted, handwritten invitation from Gabriel. Plus your helmet is still cracked, Dor. And your armor's not–"

"Oh it is SO not cracked, Kor. You don't even–"

The normally unremarkable sound of a comm buzzing hit like a table saw in Ithokor's startled ears.

"That's Uriel," Ithodor said. "I will give you a month's worth of boysenberry manna if that's not Uriel."

Ithokor turned right to look at his brother with a practiced, quick composure, belying the thoughts creeping through his heart. "So sure, are you?"

"I am. I can tell by the sound of the ring buzz."

Ithokor grimaced and furrowed his brow. "Comm signals always sound the same. So you know that's nonsensical, right?"

"Well, maybe they should be customized, Kor. There's also the fact that he normally doesn't identify himself when he calls like everybody else does. He just buzzes and doesn't say anything until we answer."

"Ithodor, how did you manage to grow a brain that's NEVER paying attention to what's in front of it?"

Their comms buzzed again.

With the window reflection showing flames in his eyes, Ithodor said, "*That's* what's in front of us now. Along with this suddenly annoying comm signal. So why don't you answer it, Captain Weirdo. And remember, a month's worth of boysenberry–"

"I heard you," said Ithokor, quickly licking his lips. "I can taste the seeds and the jelly. Get my manna ready." He raised his right forearm and clicked the channel open."

"Hello?"

<This is Uriel calling the Ith twins, do you copy?>

The Negotiator's voice boomed through the comm as he spoke, and Ithodor smiled so hard his brother thought he'd break his teeth.

"Copy sir, Ithokor and Ithodor here. How may we–"

<Get over to the Grove. Immediately. There is a major disturbance in progress, and I will need you to do your best to help quell it until I get there. If one wants to know the end, one must look at the beginning. Consider this a part of your training. Uriel out.>

The comm went silent.

"Thank you very much, have my manna delivered with extra butter, if you will," beamed Ithodor.

"I really won't. No butter for you."

"…And why not?"

"Because I never said I'd give *you* anything if I was wrong."

Ithodor blinked as he realized the correctness of his brother's words. Ithokor smirked.

"Yet another pyrrhic victory for 'Captain Perceptive.'"

"Now that's just–"

"What's 'just' is, just get ready to go. You heard Uriel."

Turn around.

It happened again. Ithodor pulled himself from the window and started pacing back and forth. He didn't want to be obviously staring at emptiness after the exchange they just had, so he stole subtle, quick scans of the room.

Still nothing.

"Oh so NOW you want to get over to that fire."

"My my, what a heel turn."

"Wait, Kor...*I'm* the one turning the heel now??"

"Well I thought you'd be rejoicing at those orders, because just seconds ago you couldn't wait to get into that blaze. This does remind me of something–I think I heard Gabriel say it once–about 'out of the frying pan.' Don't know what he was frying though. Probably okra or some such."

"Gabriel Arch Wizdor doesn't eat okra. And that other Arch Wizdor, your friend Uriel, counts this as training, huh?" said a suddenly contemplative Ithodor.

"He's your friend too, numbskull. And you're getting everything you wanted, served at light speed. Welcome to training. Welcome to an explosion we still know nothing about. And to quote someone I know that seems to master a new level of stupid every day, 'We *have* to go over there.'"

"Are endless chances to gloat all *you* want?"

Ithokor sighed. "It's not *about* what I want. Maybe one day you'll get that." Ithokor quickly glimpsed himself in the window. "Time is the last thing we need to waste. I am ready. And the state of your armor is...?"

Ithodor's face flushed a pale violet as he slightly dropped his chin and stopped pacing.

Ithokor continued. "Right. I did my armor repair the first day we got here. We are, after all, in an armory. I advised you to do the same, but that wasn't really on your agenda, was it? OooHHHH no, your list was just chock full of questioning and complaining."

Ithokor checked that his lightning sword was secured to his belt and leapt two meters into the air to stretch his arms and green-feathered wings. His tunic and golden breastplate were sealed into place as he descended to his makeshift personal locker and grabbed one of the thunderspears they'd commandeered from a Loyalist Grigori. He glowered at his wrist bruises, remembering the way he'd gotten them and the spear, but they'd healed enough to no longer bother him. Securely fastening a fresh shield onto the small of his back, the Right Twin glanced at his brother with an expression that said 'This-is-why-I'm-the-oldest.'

"Let's get ready to fly."

"…I…I need a few minutes. And by 'a few' I mean …sixty?"

"Newsflash Baron Zealous-for-Trouble, we don't HAVE a few minutes! We're going to have to go over there NOW, your damaged armor and sudden reticence notwithstanding."

Ithodor sheepishly pursed his lips as he made a spiraling column, flying straight up. He flapped his left wing vigorously, then his right one, then both together, ignoring the singed feathers that started falling off as he shook. The Left Twin felt the dents in his breastplate and his shin guards more acutely as he took practice swings with his unignited lightning sword. His left arm didn't have its full range of motion because of the warped state of his shoulder armor, and his helmet still had a huge crack in it, center right. Ithodor's skin tingled with embarrassment as he realized he'd somehow made himself look like a newborn out of the Creation Cocoons. He didn't bother to peek towards his right, knowing that the plating on his right forearm was barely hanging on.

Then it unceremoniously dropped to the floor with a clattering noise, leaving the exposed undermesh of his sleeve in its departure.

Ithokor–disapprovingly shaking his head the way a mother eagle side-eyes her chicks that won't leave the nest–stepped one meter up into the air and flew towards the door.

As the Right Twin heaved to push open the great onyx-beryl doors of the South Armory, Ithodor rapidly flightwalked over to join him mid-push. In spite of the younger brother's straining muscles pressing against the cool outer door, the zigzagged crack in his helmet, and his focused mental attempt to obey, Ithodor couldn't shake it.

He heard the voice rustling around like a drunken zephyr in his brain that wouldn't stop whispering:

Turn around.

Chapter 3

GARNISHES AND CLAPBACK
Capitulum Trēs

12:20 CELESTIAL

The Grove
Northwest Side

The thud was loud and heavy.

…It was a peach.

'Monitor untoward activity' Michael said, is what ran through Gladiator Captain L'sinell's mind right after the fruit hit him upside his head.

"Nos nihil mali fecerit," said the Dimensioner standing right in front of L'sinell. His name was Grent, and the words he spoke tumbled from his tense lips in bits and pieces. Captain L'sinell noted his speech in the Old Tongue almost as fast as he noticed the multiple fruit stains smeared all over his mouth.

Nearly half of the two hundred and fifty thousand Dimensioners were stuffing clear pouches full of as many apricots, bananas and elderberries as they could get their trembling hands on. L'sinell of the Throneists swept his gaze across them. He mushed his chrome-booted feet into the soft red grass of the Grove, steadying himself and fortifying his stance. He was a Class II Gladiator that Michael had commanded to keep order in the Realm while the Chief Gladiator himself was away on the Proxima mission. Sliding his hand very subtly toward his still-sheathed lightning sword, Captain L'sinell thought about Michael's orders as he stared at Grent the Dimensioner, whose eyes, he observed, kept flaring.

The Gladiators, Cherubim, and few Grigori that were with L'sinell, even in their peripheral, also kept seeing the Dimensioners shoving fruit down their enlarged throats so fast they were choking on it.

"Hey! We *need* that food! What the crump are you 'Bims doing?!?" A Grigori soldier two meters to Captain L'sinell's left raised both of his right arms, both hands pointing at the Dimensioners as he cried out, in a Grigori show of bravado.

The rest of his fellow Grigori nodded in agreement, but the sheepishness on their faces revealed what they were all silently thinking: *Lucifer was our Prince, and he betrayed us as well as the whole Realm, and tried to burn out our food.* Their collective shock and embarrassment was still palpable as they shook and trembled, even when reclaiming what they thought was their right.

The Throneist Cherubim that were with L'sinell felt the hair on the backs of their necks rise, raising their eye-filled wings to pre-flight position. With feathers rustling like a living red quilt, they looked like the adrenalin had not yet left their bodies from the last fight.

L'sinell motioned for his Grigori and Cherubim comrades to remain calm, but the captain kept his iron gaze on Grent.

Whatever his name is, perhaps he is their leader, L'sinell thought. *Can't confirm that assumption yet, though.*

"Non possumus facere quicquam," said Grent.

"The smoke in my face and the dented peach on the ground say otherwise," replied the gladiator captain. "And you need to speak in the Common Tongue."

Grent glanced down at the peach and then back at the captain.

"…Maybe I'll give you that one," said L'sinell, his face scrunching into a half frown as he looked at the bruised fruit. "But I am ordering you and your troops to stand down. NOW."

L'sinell knew that Grent could not possibly have thrown the peach at him, but through all the caustic smoke, the captain still couldn't tell who did. *There's a sixty percent chance it came from right behind him*, L'sinell thought, *but they're standing around in clusters. No formations.*

What the astute gladiator captain did rather clearly observe was that the Dimensioners' skin tone was markedly changing. From those in the front to some that were still flying towards the rear, the skin differentials were clear. They were comprised of Class II Cherubim, Class I and II Grigori, and even a few Class II Gladiators, and they were all growing preternaturally dark. The shades of red and blue and bronze that their epidermis seemed to be exhibiting were blackened beyond anything L'sinell had seen in his time. Their breathing as well was noticeable, as it was loud and uneven, like their lungs were frayed. L'sinell also couldn't help but detect that their eyes seemed to blink at highly irregularly timed intervals. Everything about them was eerie and wrong.

Standing in The Grove amongst the blistering fumes, facing down two hundred and fifty thousand haggardly looking Dimensioners, L'sinell could feel the growing unrest of the brethren behind him bubbling like scalding water in a cauldron. The Captain also figured getting thwacked upside the head with an oversized peach was still a pretty untoward thing.

"Nonne in idem latus Quod est quaestio hic?"

"Again. Speak in the Common Tongue," L'sinell said. "Adjust your throat reeds and we can–"

Instantly filling the air with its acrid scent, a firebomb went off to the rear. The Dimensioner Cherubim closest to Grent knocked and fired an arrow faster than L'sinell could duck. It struck the Captain in the shoulder, and a stream of his lime green blood trickled over his fingertips onto the ground.

L'sinell snap-extended the tip of his right wing and poked the Cherubim in the eye. The Dimensioner stumbled backwards, laboring even more heavily to catch his breath. For a moment, the Dimensioner Cherubim felt bile coming up and thought he would puke, but he managed to straighten up. Pure rage ran across his face.

Amidst the now yelling Grigori on both sides, the angry Cherubim rasped into Grent's ear:

"Ego sum apud te, domine. Nos es non iens retro. Et non faciet nobis."

L'sinell retracted his wing tip as quickly as he'd elongated it. Lieutenant Tull, standing on L'sinell's right, turned to the captain.

"What did he say, sir?"

"He said, 'I'm with you, sir. We are not going back. They can't make us,'" replied L'sinell. "Roughly."

"So are we just going to–roughly–let them fire an arrow at our captain and get away with it?"

"No one's getting away with anything, Tull. In fact–"

Grent struck without warning, his face darkened as he exploded directly at L'sinell. Tull leapt back as the enraged Dimensioner launched himself at the Captain, with Grent's right arm revolving around like a bizarre spinner's wheel. L'sinell sidestepped his body and avoided his whirling arm, springing back up and rotating around. Grent attacked again with the same move, right arm pinwheeling. The Throneist Captain slightly stepped to his left and ducked all in one motion, and they were back where they started. Grent's eyes had grown even wilder with curdling rage.

"I see negotiation isn't your strong suit," deadpanned L'sinell.

Grent seemed to lose what was left of his self-control, lunging at L'sinell again. He quickly mounted the same exact strike, rotating his right arm in giant circles with exasperation feeding his swings. L'sinell crushed an elbow into his side and spun fully under his arm. Grent used his wings to pivot and turned in midair to come right back at the captain. L'sinell ducked, feeling a short gust of wind as Grent's fist sailed a full two centimeters over his head.

Grent stood there, his breath coming in ragged gasps. L'sinell's gaze never broke, but he mentally clocked his opponent's lack of finesse. Desperation, confusion and some level of post-traumatic stress seemed to swirl around Grent as he readied his next move. His eyes, L'sinell noticed, conveyed the truth of having seen horrific events, but there was something else there. Something feral, fueled by adrenaline and fear. L'sinell silently thanked The Throne and Michael for their high training requirements, which he never really understood the importance of until the last week. Sweat and sinews bunched up on his arms and he tensed every muscle in his legs.

Grent abruptly spit on the ground. Then he cocked his head back and howled like a wolf whose fur was on fire.

L'sinell was momentarily startled and Grent lunged.

He scythed through the air, straining to grip L'sinell's throat. The captain dodged left and put a fist in his abdomen that landed like granite. Grent's clawing fist came swinging out right even as he doubled over from the blow, scratching L'sinell's cheek a centimeter deep. Grent hit the ground on one knee and looked like he was about to surrender…

…when he grabbed some dirt and hurled it into L'sinell's bleeding face, blinding him. Grent snapped to his feet, his left fist bashing

L'sinell's ear. The captain reeled and staggered back from the blow. Grent gathered up every drop of rage he had and followed with a mammoth right hook, landing a jawbreaker that drew more blood. Tull started to move in to defend his captain, but L'sinell through his semi-blinded haze, waved him back. Grent took a full step back to draw a breath and assess L'sinell's level of damage.

L'sinell's facial expression had not changed.

If the captain was in pain, he didn't show it. Grent swung at him four more times and L'sinell quickly arched his wings in front of his face and deflected every blow. Grent figured that his stoic foe should be unconscious or at least woozy by now from his initial connecting blows. L'sinell unfolded his wings very slowly and looked at Grent square in the eyes again. His cheek and the corner of his mouth was still dripping with lime green blood, but the captain stood like he hadn't been hit at all. Grent's furious face broke into realization, as he suddenly understood that L'sinell was just taking his measure. The Dimensioner felt his skin flush hot with fresh embarrassment and sticky rage.

Grent barked out: "*Ludis* me, gladiator? Hoc putas non est verum?"

Which roughly meant "You *taunting* me, gladiator? You think this isn't real?"

The ragged Dimensioner looked at the captain, studying new ways to try and hurt him. L'sinell slowly brought his hands up to cover his face and motioned with his right hand for Grent to come after him again.

Grent howled again as if he were turning rabid.

"I think," said L'sinell in carefully measured tones, "that maybe the confusion here is not ours."

Tull grunted. "Heh. Understatement."

Before Tull could stop smirking, Grent balanced on the balls of both feet and for a third time came straight at L'sinell. The captain feinted left as if to dodge his charge but pivoted at the last second, pounding a solid fist right into the center of Grent's chest, almost cracking his sternum. Grent felt like he'd been hit by a two-hundred-kilogram weighted slab of tungsten. The jarred Dimensioner felt the bone-to-bone contact continue to reverberate through his torso, his secondary heart racing and then fluttering like it was going to shut down. He fell back on his butt heaving, laboring to draw each subsequent breath. His cramped wings suddenly felt like he couldn't lift them, and they pulled him onto his back. Grent tried to roll to his right but couldn't, feeling his acute chest pain intensify with each second. He opened his mouth, his nose, and a few throat reeds to breathe. He fully expected L'sinell to come and deliver some sort of paralyzing blow.

"So next we're all gonna sing a worship song together or something?" said an exasperated Tull.

"'Or something,'" L'sinell said. "I'm attempting containment, Lieutenant. Out of hand is not the place to take this."

"Seems like the blood dripping on *your* hands say different. Sir."

Grent coughed and winced with pain. He glared at L'sinell and somehow found strength to spit out an insult.

"Non in ius hic es!"

"Why are you in fact shooting arrows and setting off explosions?! I have been more than patient here. And in line with Realm protocol I ordered you to adjust your throat reeds so we all can understand what you're saying equally–"

The Dimensioner immediately to Grent's right looked up and charged L'sinell, fists flailing. L'sinell was stunned at the blatant attack but quickly adjusted, feinting left. His arm a blur, he unleashed a right cross straight to his new foe's unprotected jaw. The Dimensioner's head snapped back, his body curling backward, the momentum of his assault on L'sinell springing him back like an angry rubber band. His wings not even slightly buoying him, the Dimensioner arced through the air, landing a meter away with a thudding crunch that every member of both armies felt in their bones.

Grent's troops froze and collectively held their breath for a beat…and then the front ten rows screamed with an unfamiliar battle cry. They lunged through the smoke at the Throneists and their bleeding captain, reengaging the combat anew. They fought like furious pit bulls, going for their throats with little to no concern for their own lives. As the clang and rattle of the hostile melee filled the air, Tull raised his shield and flew close to Captain L'sinell, speaking into his ear.

"This fighting sir…it doesn't make any sense."

"Tell me about it, Tull," said L'sinell, dodging another arrow. "We're supposed to be cleaning up, not still fighting. Especially with those recruited to be our *allies*. We absolutely cannot afford to lose any more food stores."

"Is that why you didn't finish him? You trying to respect the fact that they fought with us? Why are you honoring brethren that aren't honoring us?"

"Because, Tull," said L'sinell, "that is the very point of honor. It's not supposed to be conditional."

L'sinell abruptly got statue still as he focused on a strange thing unfolding in the midst of battle. Tull turned his head to the right to follow his captain's line of sight, both gladiators observing an even more worrying scene.

Not all of the Dimensioners were engaged in combat. Many of them were amazingly snarfing food. Captain L'sinell and Tull saw them filling their empty pouches and various esophagi with many foodstuffs, stopping only to fight when a Throneist engaged them.

Tull swung his shield sharply across his body, stopping three thunderspears in midair amidst looking at what he saw in their ration packs.

"You're right, Captain. We most certainly cannot afford to lose any more food stores. Or brethren. " Tull grimaced. "Still not sure how honor figures into that."

"You don't have to 'figure,' Tull!" L'sinell regathered himself after his outburst and spoke again.

"I have in fact never seen anything like this." The captain flinched as a previously ignored forearm cut started bleeding. "This situation is out of control. It needs to be contained and neutralized immediately. Because it's going to draw the worst possible kind of attention."

"And," continued L'sinell, "I don't even want to *think* about what would happen if Raphael Arch Wizdor were to show up here."

"…Why's that? I mean…Raphael is known to be the gentlest of all the Arch Wizdors."

"That is *exactly* the point, Tull. Raphael is generally non-combative. He's the last one that would want to fight, his entire focus is on keeping the brethren healthy. What do you think will happen if an Arch Wizdor with that kind of temperament sees this mess and *has* to fight?"

Tull shuddered at that thought but kept his arms moving. "Does he have a temper to lose?"

L'sinell answered back. "Do you want to find out? And see what it looks like?"

"Captain… I mean… what're we supposed to do?" as two more arrows bounced off his shield. "Contain them? Arrest them?" Tull gulped. "…*Kill* them??"

"I know what they did in helping us against Lucifer," said L'sinell. "And I know what they're doing now."

L'sinell decked another charging Dimensioner Grigori so fast the Grigori didn't have time to grunt. The Grigori slammed into one of his comrades.

"Don't you need a bandage, captain?" said Tull.

L'sinell remained silent as he realized he'd never bled so much in his existence as he had in the last week. Tull took the hint and moved on.

"So…," continued Tull, "why exactly are they still here in the first place?"

"That's the question, lieutenant," L'sinell answered. "They should all be halfway home by now."

"No, sir. I meant *here*. In The Grove. Of all places."

"Besides their obvious and completely ravenous hunger?"

The captain cocked his head as he heard more hissing to his left, like more foliage was catching fire. He fully ignited his lightning blade as the clatter of swords raged around them. "To my knowledge they were at least one million strong in that final confrontation with Lucifer. In the postlude of that fight, Ariel was kind of herding them together while Michael was getting them back to the dimensional portal he'd brought them through."

"Michael didn't feed them, sir?"

"Was their time between battle's end and portal hopping to raise a feast?" counted L'sinell.

"But where, sir? Where exactly did Michael have that portal?"

Captain L'sinell's face emoted a strange look. "You sure are picking a strange time for thirty questions. And it's not just a portal."

"What? What is it then?"

"I am not sure where it is," L'sinell sighed, ignoring Tull's last query. "Most likely somewhere near the Outlands, but that's just a guesstimate. Also. Now would be a good time to duck."

Tull barely escaped decapitation as a thunderspear whizzed over his head. He suddenly saw a Dimensioner gladiator hovering at their eleven o'clock. In one smooth motion, Tull ignited his lightning sword and threw it up at their filthy adversary, knocking a second spear out of his hand and toppling him into the burned grass.

"Good shot," said the Captain. "He's lucky to still have that hand."

"Ditto, except insert my cranium in the 'lucky-to-have' file. And did you say the *Outlands?*"

"Yes, yes, I know, Tull. But I was under the impression that the Dimensioners had all been ported back to their original planes by now. The other seven hundred and fifty thousand must've already gone through and they didn't have time for–"

Another explosion shook the ground they were standing on so hard that it ruptured right underneath their feet.

"Who keeps setting off these explosions!?" cried Captain L'sinell, as he instinctively leapt off the ground, trying to see through the smoke. He stopped at three meters into the sky, holding up his burning sword as a beacon.

Tull lifted his head up again, flapping his feathery pine green wings to clear the immediate fumes. "The smoke may be dense, but the smell of burnt fruit is everywhere, Captain. And by 'everywhere' I mean, probably in Raphael's nostrils by now."

Some of the Dimensioners seemed to laugh as their knuckles struck a bunch of Throneist Grigori jaws, splitting their blue skin right under their cheekbones from the unbridled force of the blows. L'sinell felt the still-swirling fury of the Throneists begin to rise even higher against their comrades of the last battle. Diamond swords were swinging and purple blood was splattering from increasingly tiring limbs. The Throneist Grigori noticed that even while stuffing themselves full of food, many of the Dimensioners oddly seemed to also be arguing with one another.

What kind of broken Old Tongue dialect are they speaking? Thought a large Grigori as he punched an opponent with all three arms. *And are they fighting us or themselves?*

Out of seemingly nowhere, Grent came against L'sinell one more time. He was swinging his booted toe upwards, trying to connect with the captain's chin. L'sinell instantly bent backwards ninety degrees and lifted up his legs, spring-flying parallel to the ground. Then with a split-second push of his wings he changed direction, moving forward. The captain slammed both of his feet into Grent's already broken chest, rattling the bones of his lower rib cage, sending him flying backwards. With another curt snap of L'sinell's wings, he finished his spinning kick and landed back on his feet.

Tull was watching his captain in action when he felt hot breath to his right. A Dimensioner gladiator was pushing up on him, sloshing a mouth full of spittle between snarls. The lieutenant swung his arm up, cramming his forearm between his assailant's neck and collar bone, flipping him onto his back. Their eyes met as the Dimensioner hit the ground. Tull felt anger start to cloud his vision as his adversary stared back with a desperate, unapologetic intensity. The Throneist lieutenant readied his lightning sword for what he planned on being a fight ending strike.

Wiping moist red dirt from his eye, Grent knew he couldn't get up again. He felt his vertebrosternal ribs moving with a life of their own. The soiled Cherubim stared with blazing wild eyes at Captain L'sinell, as his countenance glimmered with the dawning of a sudden realization. He held his head up as far as he could while on the ground and finally, almost defiantly, adjusted his throat reeds. Grent's fractured voice raised a question:

"You were just created in this last millennium, weren't you?"

Braced for the worst and hearing his comrade-turned-adversary speak in the Common Tongue for the first time, Captain L'sinell stood silently for a few seconds.

And, finally, he raised his hand and gestured for his troops to stand down.

"Sir!" said Tull. "That was a question, not a command for a cease fire!"

The captain ignored Tull and kept his hand raised. Only the front line was close enough to see his signal command through the smoke, so they began to fly outwards, signaling to each company to disengage and resume their formation behind the gladiator captain.

Slowly, and with much reluctance on the part of some, the Throneists began to fly back to their position behind L'sinell and stand down. The half million strong conflict in The Grove was not quickly quelled, but after waiting countless minutes, the captain heard the fighting begin to subside all around.

The acrid twang of grass and burning fruit still swirling all around them, L'sinell and Grent stood statue still opposing each other as their respective troops reassembled. Grent's bizarre inquiry had caused L'sinell's expression to become a grave question mark.

"What exactly does my creation date have to do with anything–"

"It means…" Grent continued, "you don't know about the last time we were here."

Now genuinely shocked, L'sinell shook his head in the negative.

"But indeed, if you were here before," L'sinell responded, "that makes this behavior even more mystifying. That's a one hundred percent disregard of protocols. And protocols never change."

"Heh. Spoken like a true military minion," said Grent, still coughing. "Because that's not true. I guess you weren't paying attention to what Lucifer was saying. That also means you don't know why we were…'assigned'…to those other dimensions."

"That's correct," said L'sinell. "I don't. But you fought for us. *With* us. Shoulder to shoulder. So our bound duty here should be to–"

Grent's dark face tightened into a stiff frown.

"Do not attempt to lecture me, posturing about 'duty' and 'Realm Protocols.' You know nothing. You do not even know the past that is feeding the future your polished boots are standing in this very nanosecond. But we dare not speak his name."

"Whose name? …*Lucifer's* name?" interjected Tull. "You might want to pick one subject and stay with it, Dimensioner."

"No. Not Lucifer." Grent ground his teeth. "Your MOUNTAINOUS level of ignorance notwithstanding, we are not going back. We *can't* go back."

L'Sinell, Tull, and all the brethren on the front line went quiet as they heard the determination in Grent's voice. The Throneists and the Dimensioners both stood still as the weight of Grent's words and all of the accompanying implications hung in the air heavier than the fumes they were engulfed in.

"YES! WE CAN!" A loud proclamation from Grent's right startlingly broke the silence like a rock crashing through glass. Grent couldn't hide his surprise as a Cherubim rushed over, positioning himself at his right. "And we *will* go back. All of us are not in agreement here."

Turning to his fellow Dimensioner Cherubim, Grent said, "You sure about that?"

We don't have time for dissidents, Grent thought. *This is absolutely the wrong move.*

"Just about everyone else has gone through and we are not staying here. *I* surely am not." Grent snarled, glaring at his comrade.

Taking two steps closer to them both, L'sinell sniffed the copper in the blood-filled air, clearing his throat before he spoke.

"Attention all. I do not know why you're all not with the others at the portal on your way back to your home dimensions. By my estimates, at least forty-three percent of you wish to be. Michael called you here to fight, and you've done your job. Done it well, in point of fact. Which is why I don't understand this…untoward behavior."

"What is untoward about it?" asked Grent.

"Namely," answered the captain, "your releasing of explosive charges in our food stores."

"'Our.'" Grent spat something that tasted like sputum and blueberry puree on the ground. Locking his gaze even further on L'sinell, he narrowed his eyes. "And you are assuming. Captain." Grent went into another coughing fit, feeling like he was hacking up pieces of his ribs.

"If you know my rank then obey my orders. Ariel told you what was next, Michael has gladiators running the operation to get you back home, and this dimension of the Realm obviously does not…agree with you. So why in the name of Orali are you all the way down here in The Grove stealing food?"

"*Stealing?* You think what we're doing is stealing?" Grent's grizzled visage was accompanied by even more labored and ragged breathing. "Apparently there's been some type of misunderstanding. Captain."

"Do tell, O understating Dimensioner. Is that a bona fide fact?"

"Yes. An obvious and unequivocal one. Because someone told us we could have this food."

"…*Did* they now?" countered a suddenly indignant L'sinell. He felt his right fist curl into a ball.

"And what, exactly, was this 'someone's' name?"

Chapter 4

ZEROES AND XENON
Capitulum Quattuor

12:31 CELESTIAL

The sky above the South Armory

Ithodor *turn around* found himself wishing *turn around* he had some kind of idea *turn around* what kind of life *turn around* brethren with uncluttered thought patterns *turn around* experienced.

The Ith brothers had pushed through those creaky Armory doors, letting their feet hit the lush, yellow grass. Unfurling their wings as one (a favorite twin trick of theirs), they lifted off up into the cool zephyr breezes that were common that far south of The City. The smell of the Armory's ancient metal and the freshness of the dew filled their noses as they began to pick up speed. Ithodor was scant seconds behind his brother, flying slightly erratically. He knew that his irregular flight pattern was slowing them down, and Michael wouldn't approve were he there to see it. He had trained them all better than that.

Ithodor however found that attempting to ignore his Second Sight was giving him something akin to a migraine.

Ithodor finally turned around–and saw what he thought was a statue from inside the South Armory arena–exit the building, flying away from them.

"Kor! …KOR! We have *got* to get high."

"…What *are* you babbling about–"

"We've got to arc higher and turn around. The statue… the statue… it's alive. It's one of Lucifer's troops… he was *in there with us the whole time.*"

Ithokor rolled his eyes without looking behind them. "Every *time* I think we could even smell something that whiffs like a normal life, you come up with more rubbish."

"'Normal' is relative. And boring. And this is SO not rubbish…!"

"Know what else this is not? A game. How many times do I have to tell you that? You've demonstrated enough insubordination for a millennium. Selah."

"Following one's corroborated-by-evidence hunches is not insubordination."

"Did someone alter the definition? That seems to be a thing lately."

"Yeah, well you doin' *your* thing is currently letting criminals escape."

Ithokor stayed focused on their flight to The Grove. Ithodor kept looking behind him as they flew. "It… he's getting away… what did we say in front of him…?"

"'Kor, I'm for real this time. Kor, I'm not making anything up. Kor, you have to trust me,'" Ithokor said, doing his best impersonation of his brother's voice. "Uh huh. If I had a gladiator jewel for every time you've said that to me, my wings would be as decorated as Michael's–"

Ithodor audibly caught his breath as he narrowed his eyes with a new discovery.

"There's *two* of them! Kor! He's meetin' up with a statue from the outside! WHAT in the CRUMP is even HAPPENING RIGHT NOW?"

Ithokor slowed his speed but didn't alter his trajectory one degree.

"Look bro, I supported you when you snuck, UNAUTHORIZED, into Tartarus."

"El-Adriel assisted." Ithodor smiled as he remembered all the adventures his friend had helped him with.

"So what?"

"SOOOOOO… that means there really is someone out there that believes in me. As opposed to…. y'know."

"You. Brought back. A Ravager Claw. All because of your 'mighty' intuition raves."

"That's why they call it 'intuition,' genius. Something ethereal and informative, beyond the rational mind, that's just as real as facts and logic."

"Nothing's more real than facts. Except Living Word itself, but that goes without saying. So don't say it."

"What I'm tuh-RYING to say is that I can't help it, Kor. I didn't ask for this. And this is not just intuition, I'M LOOKIN' RIGHT AT THEM. You just refuse to turn around and see what I'm seeing. But I know now like I knew then, those living Loyalist statues are on their way to spread more Death. And if you haven't noticed we survived–"

"HAH. We survived that Tartarus fiasco, Captain Frenzied Wings, because of the wisdom of Uriel. Period. Otherwise, we'd have been stripped of every jewel they have a name for and some they don't, cleaning and polishing latrines like youngling cadets. Selah squared."

"I'm NOT a 'Captain Frenzied Wings.' But I'll tell you what I am: I'm the brother that's going after those two Lucifer followers, and I'm going to bring them back. And I'll have more intel than a tub full of Cheriss. It's not just about armor being ready. It's about *us* being ready. Bruh."

"Armor? You're obsessing on that? Is that what this is about?' Ithokor rolled his eyes even harder as he began to see the faint outer edges of The Grove from their currently higher vantage point. The Right Twin also saw the billows of smoke still covering it. HIs olfactory senses began to discern faint traces of sharp steel, bleeding flesh, and burnt fruit wafting through the air.

Ithokor sighed heavily.

"Let me tell you what it's *not* about. It's never about proving things you don't have to prove, Dor."

"Or maybe you're just embarrassed that *you* didn't sense that Loyalist."

"How exactly would I have done that?"

"I don't know, Sir Nose of Mayonnaise, can't you read aura? Isn't that what your freshly minted Third Sight is?"

Ithokor's polished gold breastplate glistened even as his face flushed. "Well... yes, bro. That is correct. But number one, I don't just randomly see auras. I have to concentrate and focus to engage it. It's not on all the time. I have a mind that's perfectly capable of feeding me information without having to rely on...this kind of thing."

"And what's number two, pickle breath?"

"Hmph. Nothing wrong with a good dill for breakfast. Number two is, I'm not proud of it like you are. Because It's nothing to be proud of."

"And why not? Why *shouldn't* we be proud?"

Ithokor's unvoiced response seemed to float in the air, creating a flying silence between them so loud it threatened to crush their multi-layered ear drums. Then he spoke.

"Because, Commander Head-O'-Granite, all these extra powers, ones that the Throne may not have even wanted us to have, these powers we can't explain... correct me if I'm wrong–which is never–but wasn't having extra powers the very thing that got Lucifer into trouble?"

12:35 CELESTIAL

After four painful, conversation free minutes, Ithodor spoke again.

"I'm goin' back. I'm goin' after them. Come with me or not."

Ithodor braked in midair, almost scorching the air with his deceleration. He then arced his body like an errant kite, turned in the other direction and started to head back towards the South Armory.

"Dor! DOR!" shouted Ithokor, watching his twin fly away from him. "We're almost at The Grove! *What are you doing*??!" Ithodor grunted and turned around, kicking his speed up to try and catch up his hurrying brother.

"Whatever reason Uriel wants us there in The Grove, we need to be just that!" Ithodor shouted against the wind.

"Just what?"

"THERE!!"

"Whatever. More brethren could die if we don't catch those Loyalists."

"How does it feel, flying contrary to the wind all the time? This kind of behavior is what costs us, Dor. Costs us jewels. Rank. And reputation," said a solemn Ithokor, as the currents started pressing against his torso.

"All the more reason to hunt down and stop those that spearheaded the whole rebellion. You can still see them if you squint… there in the distance. Those Loyalists are living proof that we did not catch them all, Captain Nameless."

"I *have* a name. And I want to keep it. And perhaps brethren are dying in The Grove right now, did you consider that? I smelled something familiar that I can't quite place, but it's not good. I also think I glimpsed some of the brethren Michael called in to help us fight Lucifer's hordes over there. They're certainly… different."

"Well, good for them."

"What do you mean, 'good for them'?"

"I mean, being different is not a crime. Contrary to the belief of some that shall remain nameless. And have you thought that maybe they don't *want* to feel so different? Maybe they want to belong here, in this dimension. Maybe they want a new place to call home."

"Uh, that sounds awfully descriptive, so exactly how would you know all of that?"

"You're missing the point, Kor. That's your specialty."

"I couldn't miss the point if I dropped a mountain on top of it. That's *your* specialty."

Ithodor glared at his twin like the sun was rising behind his eyes.

"Those extra brethren should've been long gone by now. Ariel and Michael were seeing to that. And I will repeat… the *smell*…"

"What *I* smell is a chance to welcome some new brethren into The City. If they're different from the brethren we know, we should be helpin' them adjust to life in this dimension. If that isn't what being a Class I Gladiator is about, then I don't know what is. So, you go over there and do that. I'm gonna stop another insurrection before it starts." Ithodor snapped his wings like a wet towel and kicked into a high gearer, leaving his brother floating in midair.

"Ithodor! *Ithodor!*" shouted an incredulous Ithokor. "TURN AROUND! TURN! A! ROUND! COULD YOU JUST FOR ONCE NOT BE SO RECKLESS??!!!!"

Ithokor watched his words die in the air as his brother flapped his wings like they were on fire. Ithodor zoomed off like an angry Seraphim. His twin, still floating in the spot where he'd been left, pensively turned his head to look back at the smoke-filled Grove.

My brother, Ithokor thought. *My brother, my brother. Maybe I need to start coping with the idea that it's a matter of when and how. Not* if. *I have never seen impulsiveness end well for any of us. And maybe,* he pondered with a sudden shudder, *this is what Michael felt...before.*

He drew up his dark, tired wings to turn around and, with his usual resolve and resignation, headed back towards The Grove.

Again.

Chapter 5

GLORY UGLY
Capitulum Quīnque

12:42 CELESTIAL

The Sky between The Grove and the South Armory

Do you even know what's happening right now? Your brother was right about the smoke and the smell.

Ithodor's thoughts continued to trouble him, both regular and Second Sight. The canthus of his eye told him that a few hawks were soaring over the white wheat fields on his far right. He extended his scarred left arm exactly parallel to the ground he was flying over, pointing all the fingers and the thumb on his left hand in a straight line. The thick smog and burnt fruit flesh still lingered in his nose from moments ago, but he ignored those smells as the wind sizzled past him. His extreme flapping pushed his wings until the connecting tissue between his core feathered wing bones and his back began to ache.

The red-yellow grass directly beneath him almost looked like a blur, although the scruffy state of his armor did not help him aerodynamically, just like his brother had said. He wanted to just rip off some parts of his battered battle garb and hurl it to the ground, but he couldn't afford to lose even the seconds that would take.

Squinting, the Left Twin flew harder, trying to emulate the hawks he'd watched zooming over the wheat fields.

I'm not a hawk, thought Ithodor. *Because they would have more sense than to do what I'm doing. Then again maybe not.*

The bones in his vertebrae scrunched with that funny feeling that happened when he flew at high speed. The Great Hall was coming into view in his left periphery, and Ithodor tried to hide the disgust and shame he felt as he looked at the blackened heaps. What remained of the Great Hall, and the melted mass of skulls and feathers that used to be his brethren could be seen even from a distance. Ithodor also made a mental note of the legion of Messengers trying to help with the cleanup. A pungent odor punched him in the nose and he sniffled. He was close now, coming up on less than one hundred meters from the South Armory when, suddenly, he spotted them.

Ithodor saw that both of the fleeing assailants–very puzzlingly– still clearly looked like statues. They were all one golden-bronze hue, from eyes to hair to skin to armor. Looking like four buckets of fresh paint had splashed over them from head to toe, even their wings glistened with a bright copper color. Ithodor also knew what capturing these two errant combatants meant, because if the Loyalists had found a way to hide in plain sight in the Armory undetected, then Throne only knew what secrets they had been privy to. Secrets that were spilled by anyone coming to access the scores of Armory weapons, unaware that they had eyes on them. Said weapons also including the revamped and upgraded units Michael hadn't made public yet.

Yet another thing that I shouldn't know. Something Uriel strangely made me and Kor aware of. Ithodor squinted again.

Oh, how I wish I had Gabriel's ears right about now. I need to know what they're saying.

The Left Twin dug his nails into his palms, feeling his sweat stream off of him. Their flight patterns were erratic to the extreme, almost like a flying version of stuttering.

Then *they* saw *him.*

If pseudo-animated statues could disgustingly flash horror, shock and anger across their refined faces, these Loyalists did just that.

One Loyalist flew straight up without missing stride, straight towards the sun. The other one, the one he recognized from inside the gym, turned full speed to his left at a hard perfect ninety-degree angle.

That's impossible, thought Ithodor. *Nobody could even attempt a turn like that. Except Gabriel, perhaps. And, Throne help me, I have to catch them before they can get back to…wherever they're going.*

The Loyalist tore off even faster down towards the Forever Forest. *He can't be going in there. I can't possibly follow him if he does. I've got maybe one shot at stopping him, and it's going to hurt.*

Ithodor took a quick glance behind him, squinting into the sunlight to see if he could spot the other Loyalist. He thought that his escape vector of flying straight up was dumb, as it would enable him to be more easily spotted.

He saw nothing except a lone eagle, casually making his way east. The Loyalist had disappeared. He turned back to the opponent in front of him, realizing that at the speed he was flying, the increased wind shear would serve as an advantage.

This move is the specialty of both the Messengers and the Seraphim, thought Ithodor.

As a Gladiator, Ithodor didn't have nearly their level of vocal power or skill. But if he didn't go for it, the statue-faced Loyalist would escape, maybe even into the Forever Forest. Which meant that no one would ever find him again.

With the wind whipping around and through him, Ithodor inhaled, hurting his chest as he did. And then he screamed.

The sonic attack launched from his throat reeds. It came out in a much wider cylindrical pattern than either a Messenger or a Seraphim would've done. The beam wasn't nearly as tight or as focused as it should be. It lacked the full punch of the other classes, and Ithodor felt his throat start to shred.

In seconds, the sonic beam hit his quarry squarely on his thighs and on the joint of his wings as they flapped. It was enough to knock him to the ground and give Ithodor the moment he needed to catch up to him. The Loyalist tumbled several times on the ground, knocking his mask off. He was still face down when a wheezing Ithodor finally flew upon him. The young warrior drew his lightning sword and pointed its crackling tip at his downed opponent.

Ithodor saw that his enemy's true hair was matted and splotchy, and again marveled at the level of detail that went into the statue disguise.

"You…are…under arrest," squeaked Ithodor. *Throne preserve me. I can barely talk.*

"Am I, buddy?" his adversary replied, his voice clearly smirking. "That was a nice trick with the sonics." He unhurriedly turned his face around and stared Ithodor right in the eyes.

Ithodor's brain went into shock, the kind where truth and facts are moving through the synapses at meteoric speed, but the soul doesn't want to accept the information. Or process it. The stunned gladiator-in-training blinked twice, realizing exactly whose face he was looking into:

The face of a friend.

"El-Adriel?" said Ithodor, hurting his throat even further. "You're a LOYALIST?"

El-Adriel fully turned his body to face his captor. Relaxing his verdant wings, he sat on his butt and cocked his head at Ithodor. With the disguise peeling away, Ithodor saw that El-Adriel's skin had become slightly chalky, with his hands and feet reflecting very dark hues of red and black. The former friends just stared at each other for uncountable seconds, neither flinching, moving, or breaking their gaze.

"I…I don't know what I am," El-Adriel finally said. "It's not like I signed up or anything. All I know is that I'm better than I was before."

"What…what exactly does *that* mean?" asked a still stupefied Ithodor, unwillingly remembering better days.

"It means, buddy, that I had heard how Lucifer had gotten his additional abilities. The Realm was literally buzzing with the truth of what he'd done." El-Adriel tensed his legs, as if he were going to spring up, but in spite of his pain Ithodor stayed visually locked onto him.

"There were too many corpses on the field, I didn't even think anyone would notice! Yeah, I broke protocol, so what? …There was so much noise, I figured one time wouldn't hurt, I…"

"So you…you drank of the inscriptions of others? Of your fallen brethren?" said Ithodor.

"I can *fly*, Ithodor. And I mean really move, like a peregrine falcon. I can aviate at speeds that gladiators can't even dream of!"

"Which is what happens when you drink the inscriptions of others," Ithodor said, coughing.

"You make it sound like it's a bad thing. A Seraphim that defected to Lucifer's side died right in front of me."

"So your response was to ingest his inscriptions? Just like that?" Ithodor asked, with no attempt to hide the disgust in his voice.

"I had nothing to lose."

"Except everything you used to stand for," said Ithodor.

"Ithodor… you are nothing but what you have always been: a ridiculous idealist," argued El-Adriel.

"No…no." Ithodor coughed and spit, his voice was nearly gone.

"I've always known that nothing is as it seems." Ithodor's nose began to bleed. "That's not idealism, it's a commitment to realism. Which always seems to be the minority opinion."

He found himself shaking his head at his former friend.

"I absorbed inscriptions. It happened. And here's another newsflash for your naïve little soul…

I liked it. Didn't you see? Can't you see what's right in front of you, Ithodor? I was turning at right angles! You *saw* me! We get more powers, you idiot! Can't you see that? Lucifer did.

WHY CAN'T YOU SEE THAT WE GET MORE POWERS?"

El-Adriel's eyes flared as he smiled again. "And since you clearly won't be making with the sonics again anytime soon…." He subtly let his wings unfurl into pre-flight position.

The now silent gladiator stepped right into his friend's face without dropping his guard, keeping his lightning sword trained on El-Adriel's throat. Ithodor's larynx and his soul were in far too much pain for him to give utterances, but he did allow his eyes to glance at El-Adriel's discolored extremities.

The cornered dark gladiator followed Ithodor's pensive gaze. "Yeah yeah, there's a cost…so what? I'm willing to pay it to realize my potential, that's the difference between you and me."

Ithodor rolled his eyes. The irony of El-Adriel's statement hurt his capillaries.

"So, I'm sure you're wondering what we were doing in the Armory. Well, one of Lucifer's Kroni saw me right after the Inscription

Transfer happened and brought me these clothes. And that mask. And some paint. That doesn't make me a Loyalist, Ithodor… it makes me someone whose had his eyes opened to the truth."

Ithodor curled his face into a mask of anger.

El-Adriel did the same, yet his anger was plastered on his countenance with smugness paint.

They dropped into a low squat, both bending their knees while keeping their torsos upright. There was a slight shuffling of feet as the proper stances danced on their toes in anticipation.

El-Adriel swiftly drew his sword up over his head and cranked it down towards Ithodor. Ithodor rotated his sword around sideways, positioning the handle higher than usual, creating something akin to a lightning roof above his face.

El-Adriel's blow bounced off the crackling roof like hail, as Ithodor sidestepped him, sizzling his sword down toward his unprotected shoulder. El-Adriel took a glancing blow, as Ithodor's strike was slightly off the mark. El-Adriel felt a small chunk of his right shoulder pad and his right cheek get seared off. He continued laughing.

They rebalanced and faced each other again. El-Adriel couldn't keep the curiosity off his face, wonder why his now former friend would be resisting him instead of joining him.

El-Adriel attacked again in a more linear manner. He spread out to stand on the edges of his feet and did a quick snap cut in the direction of Ithodor's throat. Ithodor barely parried it and took one step back.

The gladiator twin knew that this would be a moment for a skull-busting wail, but his throat hadn't nearly recovered enough. He jerked and popped his blade at El-Adriel, but his opponent kept parrying his attack like he had caught Ithodor's rhythm and flowed in time with it. Ithodor caught a whiff of the corpse scent on his opponent and realized that he was more interested in humiliating him than beating him.

"I'm going to drink from your inscriptions too, old friend," said El-Adriel. "As well as from your blood. And I'm going to drink both quite deeply."

Ithodor's hurting larynx let his facial expression respond.

You'll have to leech it out of me first, you sick traitor.

Even in the midst of an off-balance sword fight exacerbated by an aching throat, Ithodor suddenly understood: attempting to reason with El-Adriel would be futile. He couldn't understand his former friend's side of things, and El-Adriel was having none of his.

The newly minted Loyalist sneered and waved his hand towards Ithodor with a motion that said, 'come on.'

El-Adriel reached again to his hip, his fingers wrapping comfortably around the scratched hilt of his sword. He sprung forward, cutting upwards at Ithodor, and then changed his motion mid-strike to a forty-five-degree angle. Ithodor was caught off-guard by the multi-angled attack but was still fast enough for the blow to miss him left, glancing off his shoulder, drawing sparks from his armor. El-Adriel snarled with irritation; he thought this would be over much more quickly. Ithodor briefly rolled his eyes as he heard his brother's voice in his head, lecturing him about protocol-ready armor.

El-Adriel quickly cut again, down and across from his right shoulder, with clear sights on Ithodor's face. The brash twin lurched back, with his opponent's blade coming within a centimeter of his nose. El-Adriel took advantage of his off-balance position, reversing his next attack with an attempt to take Ithodor's head completely off.

Ithodor surprised him by ducking, feinting left, and then unleashing the mother of all uppercuts onto El-Adriel's surprised jaw. The connecting blow knocked him back on his rear, and the irate

Junior Gladiator stuck his pulsating sword right underneath his friend's chin. He looked down at him and mouthed the word, 'talk.' Followed by 'right now.'

El-Adriel chuckled as he spit two teeth out of his mouth. "That was quite a blow there, junior. Somebody's been teaching you how to fight. You know the Kroni that talked to me, he told me to go to the Armory and blend in as a statue for as long as possible. He also said I'd receive further instructions later." He wiped at the stream of blood trickling out of the right side of his mouth, softly chortling again.

Is this later? Scrolled across Ithodor's face. For a split-second he adjusted himself to mouth some questions to El-Adriel–

–when a sheet of pure copper flame erupted between them and knocked Ithodor back. With his gladiator tunic catching fire around his shoulders, Ithodor started quickly patting his arms to try and extinguish the flame. It burned fast and started to burn through in seconds.

El-Adriel jumped straight up into the air and rocketed west along the perimeter of the Forever Forest. He turned a corner, but Ithodor couldn't tell if he went into the Forest or not. He cocked his wings as if to shift them into a higher gear, and like that, Ithodor's friend-turned-Loyalist was gone.

Ithodor brought his wings into forward position and started rapidly flapping them to snuff out the flames that were stinging his skin like a crab's pincers. His voice was shot.

How in the world am I going to tell Ithokor what's happened? He realized that the far-reaching implications of what El-Adriel had confessed to him were game changing for the entire Realm. *And it's going to freak my already meticulously apprehensive brother out. Write that in gold.*

It was at that precise moment he looked on the ground and saw what he caused the flames that distracted him. Ithodor realized in a moment of time what must've happened to cause those explosions in The Grove. Both queries, El-Adriel's escape distraction, and the fires in the food stores, had the same answer:

Brimstone.

The Mole

The mole settled in as he had been trained to, opening his senses to everything that was happening around him. Every sight, sound, and smell began to pour into his overworked hippocampus, and he catalogued everything almost immediately. That brain of his had always been a bragging feature, and now it felt like another shackle around his neck.

His amygdala was telling him however that *it* was nowhere near death. He had hoped that as time went on he could adjust to what he was doing, as he felt like he had no choice. Something in him reminded him that he'd always had a choice, but he crushed that inkling and kept absorbing sensory data.

He knew that one day really soon, this would all be over, but two things about that truth plagued him:

One, 'soon' is forever a relative term. And two, it was possible that the aftermath of his current actions would bode worse for him, carrying a fate that was incomprehensibly terrifying.

Although, it was my previous actions that got me here, he thought. *And the name that I believed in.*

And apparently…I can't unburn those memories from my brain.

Chapter 6

DROSS POINT EDITS

Capitulum Sex

12:30 CELESTIAL

The Grove
Northwest Side

"Him."

L'sinell looked skyward to where Grent was pointing and saw something he didn't expect to see: the Right Twin Ithokor arching his smooth green wings into landing position to genteelly begin his descent.

There are quite a few of those extra brethren here, thought Ithokor, *but less than those that fought with us in battle. And that's a good thing, they don't belong here permanently. How can* they *not know that?*

Ithokor swirled through the smoke and touched down without sound to Captain L'sinell's right. He quickly saluted, simultaneously folding his wings into his back. Tull stood silently on his captain's left, watching the gladiator twin with a hawk-like gaze.

Ignoring the stinging in his nostrils, Ithokor saw the fresh blood and half-eaten fruit scattered across the grassy red terrain. Dirty fire still burned to the rear of both camps and the chalky soot started to coat his tongue. The Right Twin, however, continued standing at attention before L'sinell. The astonished gladiator captain, without blinking, returned his salute, and slowly turned his gaze back to Grent.

Grent peered through the ever-swirling smoke, looked at L'sinell and nodded in the affirmative.

"He's the one who told us we were welcome to this food."

"…I beg your pardon?" said an astonished Ithokor. "Is there a problem, sir? I'm here to help."

The loudest sound anyone heard was the scarred lung breathing of all the Dimensioners before Captain L'sinell opened his mouth to speak.

"'Problem' is the most relative term in all of the known languages of The Realm, Junior grade. And whether or not that's what we have here… that has everything to do with your next answer."

Ithokor thought he felt a bug in his ear. *Must've picked that up when I pulled into the sky here. Of course, I have a bug in my ear, why wouldn't I have a bug in my ear?* He did his best to ignore it.

L'sinell leaned in until he was scant millimeters from Ithokor's flushed face.

"Did you, or did you not, tell these *Dimensioners* that they could eat all this food in The Grove?"

"Unequivocally not," said Ithokor without hesitation. "I am not acquainted with these brethren in the slightest. Nor do I understand why they're here."

Grent cocked his head to the right, unable to hear the hushed conversation. His voice was still shaky but sarcasm seemed to give it strength. "If he's telling you he doesn't know us, then green wings there seems to have a mighty short memory."

Ithokor fired back with enough volume for the entire front line to hear him. "You can't remember a conversation you never had, brother... whatever your name is. And I would never endorse any orders that went against Michael's directives. Both Michael and Ariel were clear. You, *Dimensioners*, should've been back in your own spaces by now. Where you obviously belong."

L'sinell swept his eyes right to study a nervously indignant Ithokor for a half second, then returned his gaze to Grent.

"If junior grade here says he didn't do it, then he didn't do it. You lot are lying. Which is something that someone apparently convinced you was okay to do."

Ithokor nodded. "And clearly what's needed here is a return to Michael's solid exit plan, to relocate all of you to your respective dimensions of origin, and out of The Grove. Away from our food stores."

"It took us hours to get here from that wretched Dimensional Gate," said Grent. "And there were problems there, green wings. *Severe* ones."

"You are a bold-faced liar!" shouted Tull.

"And that," continued L'sinell, "leads me to believe that maybe you're reconsidering your position in this conflict."

If undrawn lightning swords had a pre-ignition crackle, every soldier in The Grove felt like they heard it.

And then a thought hit Ithokor, so simple and yet so logical:

"Maybe it was my brother," he whispered, in that I-hope-you-hear-me-'cause-I-don't-want-to-own-this kind of way.

"Excuse me, what did you say?" asked L'sinell. Their tones were suddenly fiercely hushed again, causing Grent to strain to hear what they were saying, but to no avail.

Ithokor moved uncomfortably close to L'sinell's ear, until the captain could smell the last banana Ithokor had eaten.

"I said...sir...that maybe he's referring to my brother. My drama loving, trouble sniffing twin."

"Twin, you say? Where is he then?"

"He's...ah...well, south of here. Chasing a long story."

"How in the name of Orali would a junior grade gladiator even have the *authority* to grant access to The Grove? And what does 'chasing a long story' mean?"

"It means I could elaborate on what he's chasing, but that's a... rather long story."

The sounds of skirmishing and struggling came nearer to where L'sinell, Tull and Ithokor were standing and whispering.

Before L'sinell could respond he heard:

"Get OFF me–"

"Quare non solum nos relinquere tu?"

"I told you to let go!"

"Nos erant manducare permissum ipsi erat iste!"

Finally, three blue figures emerged from the smoke.

"'Operation: Retrieve' underway," said the lead Grigori to Tull. "We've successfully begun to wrestle some of that stolen food from them."

"Excellent," said Lieutenant Tull. "Get it out of here and back to Raphael's storehouses for safe keeping. Keep your movements on the ultra-quiet." The Grigori nodded and padded their heavy, three-armed frames out of Tull's sight, back into the fog.

Ithokor looked astonishedly at L'sinell. "When did you...? I mean, you've had an operation running since I've been here?"

"That's one thing you're top notch at, junior grade. Being a distraction." Ithokor blinked at Tull as he and L'sinell turned to face each other, still keeping their voices low.

Grent had been slowly creeping closer to L'sinell and the Throneists, but incrementally so. He yelled out to Ithokor. "What happened to all your talk of welcoming us to this dimension?"

"That. Wasn't. Me." grunted Ithokor, through gritted teeth.

"Really, green wings? How are you going to disprove my claim when myself and several other brethren saw you with our own multi-eyes?"

Ithokor sprung up precisely two meters off the ground. Out his periphery he saw the Throneist Grigori moving in groups of three on the Dimensioners. The Grigori were moving slowly, sometimes snatching the satchels of fruit from their adversaries before they knew what happened. Ithokor reasoned they had just a few scant seconds before this operation reached the ears of Grent.

Yelling at Grent, Ithokor said, "Everything isn't as it seems."

Grent yelled back, "That's a very tired cliché. Too bad the facts say otherwise."

Grinding his teeth, Ithokor flightwalked backed to L'sinell and Tull and leaned in to hear what they were discussing. Speaking up he whispered, "I have an idea. It will require your best fliers. How many do you have?"

L'sinell harumphed and asked, "When did you junior grades get so... full of yourselves? Interrupting the conversations of senior officers?"

"I'm not- sir, I meant no disrespect. I just mean that we are eventually going to have to get these Dimensioners out of here. We don't want Raphael himself to come down here because that will be an automatic writeup on our records, regardless of the outcome. Plus, Throne only knows what else."

"You don't have to instruct me on the gravity of the situation, gladiator. I'm well aware."

Ithokor nodded with a subtle bow. "Uriel may or may not be coming, you know that the Negotiator would never write us up if he could help it. So we need to handle things in case Uriel never makes it. And if a distraction is what you need, I've got just the thing."

"You mean, you have both an extraction *and* a distraction idea?" asked Tull.

"Yes to both, sir," Ithokor said, craning his neck to look skyward. "As you said...it's what I'm good for."

It was less than five seconds later when sheepishly, roughly, with unkempt wings and a face aching from being burned, Ithodor landed next to his brother. The still billowing smoke had coalesced around them again, obscuring the Left Twin's arrival from Grent and the Dimensioners. Ithodor's eyes were screaming as he landed, wide as saucers from his ordeal. His brother had as usual sensed his imminent arrival but quickly noticed that he was uncharacteristically silent.

"What's wrong?" asked Ithokor.

Ithodor mouthed the words:

[I can't speak. My throat reeds are raw.]

"What happened back there?"

[I know you're thinking it's bad. It's not.]

Ithodor held his head down.

[It's worse.]

"This is *not* the time for your smart mouth, O king of understatement. Even if I can't actually hear it." Ithokor wondered if his Third Sight would help in this situation, loath as he was to us it. The captain's voice interrupted his pondering.

"Answers." L'sinell spat through pursed lips.

"I need them. Not your private twin communiqués."

"As I said, I think that we can–"

"Why are you even here?" blurted out Tull.

"We're *supposed* to be here, sir," said Ithokor. "We were ordered to be here."

"By the very Arch Wizdor you say may not even be gracing us with his presence, correct?"

"Well…yes."

And what have you brought with you since you've been here, junior grade?" said Tull.

"I…"

"Uh huh. The correct answer is 'zero.' Don't hurt your brain trying to count that high."

Ithokor turned to fiercely stare at his unshaven brother with a look only twins could understand or perceive. He was searching his face for the truths his brother's tongue couldn't convey.

"IF you two are DONE with your twin bonding," grunted L'sinell, "I've got a MILITARY OPERATION here that's about seventy-eight degrees turned on its head. We REALLY DON'T–"

It was at that moment that the Dimensioners struck.

Quick bursts of copper smoke started popping all around where the Captain, Tull, and the twins were standing. The Throneists behind them started scrambling as L'sinell yelled, "Wind attack. Every wing available. Do it NOW!"

The air started buzzing with the monstrous sound of a quarter million plus wings starting to flap at high speed. Grent turned around to his troops and said,

"Now's our chance. Gather whatever fruit you have left and we will break out of here towards the south."

"But sir… won't they just follow us?"

"No," smiled Grent, "because their wings will be too tired to keep up."

L'sinell realized that it wasn't just the sound of their rapidly moving wings he was hearing. His opponents were actually chanting.

"Aedes Michaelis nunc est nostra domus! AEDES MICHAELIS NUNC EST NOSTRA DOMUS!"

Tull turned to L'sinell. "Are they saying what I think they're saying?"

L'sinell reluctantly nodded. "Something to the effect of…'Michael's house is now our home.'"

The Dimensioners did not lift off vertically. They started dashing and darting at higher and higher speeds on horizontal vectors as they chanted. They moved into thirty-degree angles, moving and then snapping back into their original place, like angry rubber bands. And their wings became more and more transparent as their flap velocity started to increase.

L'sinell wasn't sure what to expect. He tensed his thigh muscles, tightening a sweaty grip on his sword, preparing for a multi-directional onslaught that his troops may indeed have been too tired to withstand. The thrumming in the air built to a frenzied crescendo…

…When a booming baritone sound resonated from the sky. A voice that none of the combatants expected to hear.

"You. are not. Going. Anywhere." The voice tensely paused, as if waiting for the many buzzing wings to subside.

"*None* of you are."

L'sinell heard that voice and felt his hand involuntarily spasm. Ithokor saw his reaction and strained to see the source of the piercing voice. Ithodor just leaned on his brother and sighed.

And then Ithokor saw clearly who it was.

"Oh, my holy manna," the Right Twin said.

"It's Raphael."

Ithodor's throat still aching, he strained his neck skyward to behold Raphael pull out the purest colored cobalt blue sword he'd ever seen. There seemed to be something crackling in and around the blade, but it wasn't lightning. The Left Twin wasn't sure what it was.

Electromagnetic waves emanated from the pulsing sword, as Ithodor felt something akin to the pre-rumble tremors a groundquake makes.

And then, he felt nothing.

Every single soldier on both sides of the conflict felt nothing.

Nothing at all.

Chapter 7

EMIT EMIT EMIT

Capitulum Septem

Billowing, flowing, fluidic acerbic smells of regurgitated dahlia shaped wormhole strings blended into heterogenous, amalgamated blinding kaleidoscopic warping blues, greens, and yellows. Spinning concentric soundwave wheels turned chartreuse, then into rose cherry crimson oblong megahertzal silky strands of rippling, interplexing reality breakers arching in quartal prisms through a freezingly broken sky.

Wind sped up as it slowed down to gush east and west at once upending gravitational norms. Blocks of Skydrip started cascading upward and thinning out as it crawled higher. Spoken words being formed in the throat reeds of all brethren slowed to a crawl and then become StillWord sounds, syllables formed but not uttered. Limbs and wings that could move at blinding speeds felt like molasses and plastic as bones, joints and ligaments ground to a halt, with red, purple, green and blue blood-based circulation systems losing their ability to transport oxygen or the various parts of hemoglobin required to stain the blood with its color.

Perception in over half a million brains went from film cells to still pictures as the very sight and scope of Raphael's BlueSword swelled into one million reflections of itself, living only in the peripheral vision of all who saw it. Light continued to splinter in chronometric waves that caused the memories of the current battle to look like echoes of dead time wrapped in past synaptic spirals, effectively merging minutes with hours with days in gloppy, heavy curdles that made brains feel like noodles and noodles feel like music.

Raphael Arch Wizdor had used his Blue Chronosword to stop time, and the only Arch Wizdor with topaz eyes already felt the cost of doing so crawling across his lower spine.

Every brother knew that Raphael was the Arch Wizdor not given to temper. So their arrested irises, lenses, and corneas registering his flushed faced and raised voice created an etched series of pastel snapshots that were already burning their way indelibly into their seized craniums.

"What. Is. The. Meaning. Of. All. Of. This," Raphael thundered. To his right and to his left were his medical aid teams, clad in their normal white robes with sky blue trim around every cuff and hem and line. Their faces were customarily neutral, although further scrutiny would reveal the shock they were attempting to mask.

Raphael knew that it was ridiculous to expect an answer with all of the brethren in their altered state. He held his Chronosword high, seemingly standing in the moment. He let the weight and heat of his disdain hang in the air like the humidity of a long summer, so that every Throneist and every Dimensioner could feel it. The Arch Wizdor of Healing felt the coughing stirring in his trachea and the nausea building in his stomachs, reflexively knowing that he was in for a very rough couple of days after this.

Minutes and seconds that were impossible to measure passed, as there was now no time flowing in the embattled Grove area at all. Raphael moved his arm from holding his Chronosword high and pointed it at L'sinell. There was a loud *snap* like the sound a rubber band makes when its breaking point has been reached, and Captain L'sinell fell to the ground. He began to wretch and heave, drawing air back into his lungs, yet feeling vomit begin to trickle up his esophagus and erupt onto the ground.

"You will give me a full disclosure explanation of this travesty," said Raphael, "or Peripheral Edema and Tachycardia will be the least of your worries."

"Yes…yes sir," said L'sinell, amidst his hacking and puking. "The long and short of it is that these brethren that Michael brought in to help us fight Lucifer are in the wrong. They thought they could help themselves to as much food in the Grove as they wanted. They claimed they were authorized to do that by…"

The twins gulped.

"By parties unknown. They were then Brimstone fighting anyone who tried to say otherwise."

"Oh really?" intoned Raphael.

The Healer moved his arm again and pointed the terrible Chronosword at Grent. There was again an ear-piercing *snap* and Grent fell to the ground. He too began to wretch and heave, but almost began convulsing from the heavy damaged he'd already sustained from the fight.

Grent choked out his words.

"I thought…I thought you were supposed to be the Healer of the brethren," he said.

"I am," said Raphael without moving. His voice seemed to rumble at frequencies they felt rather than heard. "I am also Guardian of the Grove and everything in it. You will answer me as to why you were here taking food."

"After the…after the battle with Lucifer and his Loyalists," Grent said, coughing out each sentence, "we were told by one of those gladiator twins that we were welcome to refresh ourselves here in the Grove. And that he was sure Uriel or one of you Arch Wizdors would support us staying in this dimension."

Raphael turned his penetrating gaze to the Twins and locked on to their time-frozen countenances. He could see with his Health Vision that Ithodor's throat was wounded.

"There was an operation in place to summarily return these brethren to their respective domiciles, so abrogating that edict was a spontaneous decision by one person?"

L'sinell and Grent, without looking at each other simultaneously answered Raphael:

"Apparently so."

A curious expression crept its way across Raphael's face, but he remained silent. He slowly pointed his pulsating sword at Ithodor and waved it. The cobalt energy surged toward the frozen twin, and Raphael broadened the twist of his wrist to include Ithokor in the sweep. The twins finished the sentences and flightwalking they were doing before Raphael arrived, and simultaneously fell to the ground like puppets whose strings had been abruptly cut.

Ithokor recovered first and looked around him, staring at the myriad numbers of immobilized brethren. Slowly, as his lungs felt like needles were clawing at them, he stood back up. The Right Twin reluctantly turned to face Raphael, his vomit spittle still hanging off the right side of his trembling mouth. "Raphael...sir...I believe this has been a terrible misunderstanding."

"What you believe is irrelevant. What you've done is at hand."

"It wasn't...I mean...my brother didn't think he was authorizing anything. I believe he just mentioned to them that there was an abundance of food in the Grove, and they–"

Raphael's eyes narrowed. "I can see the damage to his throat reeds. It is extensive, so I will take that as the reason he is not speaking for himself. But 'accidently authorizing' a raid that's cost lives, resources and time–as well as furthering the existence of an already tense climate–is the most ridiculous thing my ears have heard today. Many of our Realm Bistros have been levelled, do you understand that? There is an unprecedented number of brethren with specific wounds that need attending. And I'm looking at brethren immature enough to think that there aren't bigger things happening here than their alimentary canals."

Ithokor seemed to take that last comment literally and grabbed his abdomen.

"I…I am actually in agreement with Captain L'sinell," said Ithokor, still coughing. "I believe the Dimensioners have no right to be here and should've followed the post-battle protocol and gone back home as instructed."

Raphael pointed his mysterious blue sword at Tull, dissolving the time stasis around him like ice cream on a hot day. Tull had the longest time of recovery of anyone that Raphael had released. Raphael waited patiently for the Dimensioner to gather enough air back into his pain wracked lungs to speak.

"I will not bore you with flowery speeches, Raphael Arch Wizdor. Some of the Dimensions we come from are quite restrictive. Many of them do not boast the splendor, the resources, or the opportunities that this one, the one you Arch Wizdors live in, does. Some of us, the oldest among us, have been there since Millennia Past. And the dimension transfer process is painfully unpleasant. Many of us do not want to go back. We…we *cannot* go back."

Raphael's face remained inscrutable but his thoughts raced faster than angry lightning.

Tull relayed his position, and the Arch Wizdor took a deep breath and spoke.

"You forget who you are speaking to, Tull. I wanted to hear your perspective in your own words for the official record. But I know *why* you and your fellow Dimensioners were reassigned to those Dimensions, remember? Maybe your memory is fuzzy."

"Or," continued Raphael, "maybe you thought your attempt at revisionist history would carry a modicum of weight here. But in this current situation, or any other, the Arch Wizdors never forget. We were there. That's why this foolish attempt to stay here is an insult to our collective intelligence."

Grent's face again twisted into a mask of rage.

"Ah yes, the high and mighty Arch Wizdors. The one class of brethren that continues to believe in the Old System. And why wouldn't you, as it always keeps you in power. Your memories are long because anything other than status quo means the end of you."

"I am unmoved by your insults," Raphael said. "As with all of the dissidents around here lately, you think it is the first time I have heard such accusations, tinged with the false syrup of bitterness. I have responsibilities larger than you can possibly fathom."

L'sinell, still stunned by the hubris Grent had in speaking to Raphael, stared intently into the Arch Wizdor's burning topaz eyes. "Not all of them want to stay, sir, from what we heard. Is there a backstory here that we don't know about, sir? How do you know–"

"Since they're all time frozen, can't we just... fly them back to the Dimension Portal?" interjected Ithokor. "Wouldn't that solve our current problem?"

"That would take double the resources if I had to assign someone to guard and transport every one of these Dimensioners," said Raphael. "And we don't have that kind of time. I'm going to have to unfreeze them and direct them to go back under their own power."

L'sinell was again stunned. "You're going to trust Grent to...follow orders?"

"He will not have a choice if he wants to live," answered Raphael. "Have you not noticed the effect that the air here is having on them?"

L'sinell nodded with the hesitancy of sudden realization.

"Now that you voice it, sir…yes, I have."

Ithokor tried to control his reaction as well, but he couldn't. He recoiled in horror at Raphael's words. "Sir, if you look closely, some of the brethren have turned fully two dimensional. They now only have height and width. What's going to happen to them if they come out of time stasis like that?"

Raphael looked up as if he hadn't heard Ithokor.

"It is beyond amazing how no one listens to counsel until there is a crisis. A crisis that could have been averted by application of the aforementioned listening."

The quietly angered Arch Wizdor tried to hide his reluctance. He straightened his torso and breathed deeply, slowly waiving his sword across the emblazoned Grove area. It was halfway through that process when his communicator buzzed.

He looked onto his wrist comm, tapped his earpiece and whispered, "Raphael."

On the other end of the buzz was Uriel.

Uriel spoke in uncharacteristically hushed tones. He spoke quickly and succinctly, which let Raphael know he was beyond serious in his communication. The conversation was less than five minutes long, but its implications could be felt in the air around the Arch Wizdor. Raphael nodded precisely one time and turned his comm off.

Without hesitation he looked at the only brethren around him stirring, as the multitudes of time arrested brethren stayed unmoving. "There is new information," Raphael said. "Its dissemination will have to wait until everyone in this Grove is again active." Raphael drew an even deeper and longer breath as he again raised his Blue Chronosword above his curly brown head…

And his comm flared to life again.

Raphael sighed and looked down. His eyes quickly indicated that this call was even more serious than the last, because it was on an encoded frequency that only the Arch Wizdors could hear. He tapped his earpiece three times to connect to that frequency.

The caller was Michael.

Chapter 8

OPPOSITE ZERO
Capitulum Octo

"Can you hear me clearly?" asked Michael.

"Yes," said Gabriel, many light years away. Uriel, in his mansion, also answered in the affirmative. Raphael floating above the still burning Grove nodded his head until he realized Michael couldn't hear a head nod and said, "Loud and clear."

"Good," said Michael with no hint of a smile in his tone. "Because you'd better. I've been getting reports about the Grove, and what these so-called Dimensioners have been doing. You three need to know that… I invoked something older than we are to get that Dimension Gate open the first time. I asked to open the Scrolls of Sephiara."

"You did *what?*" said Gabriel, whisper-yelling at Michael's statement.

"You heard me. It's one of the few scrolls that we can access that can affect time and space. It was necessary because of the level Lucifer took things to. I shouldn't have to explain that part."

His brothers' silence let Michael know that they understood, even if they didn't fully agree.

"There's a problem at the Dimensional Gate because of who the Dimensioners are, and the Sephiaraic Scrolls knowing that. It's why they can't just fly back through. Their connection to *the Unspeakable* is causing a monstrous feedback loop. Certain time and space dimensions don't want to bend back open to let them in. Again."

"So, what are we to do?" asked an unusually somber Uriel.

"A bunch of things we don't wanna do, Uriel. I will take point since I got us into this. It is costing massive amounts of energy to keep that gate open, on top of what it cost through the Scrolls to get it open in the first place. And all of it predicated on the condition that they would go back after the fighting was done. They *can't* stay here or…" Michael's voice trailed off.

"Or what?" demanded Gabriel.

"Or there's going to be great personal sacrifice," answered Michael.

"Add to that, that the air here cannot sustain them," intoned Raphael.

"Affirmative," answered Michael. "I'm on my way to petition The Throne personally. And directly. And yes, I'm going by myself. The arguments I can already hear forming in your brains are moot. What's done is done. And the clock is ticking."

Whispering so low that the Grove combatants around him couldn't even hear his whispers, Raphael said:

"What if it's not that simple? Uriel can attest to this situation's lack of simplicity, as It was apparently his trainees that caused it."

"I knew it," said Gabriel. "I just knew it."

"How is *not* simple, Raphael?" said Michael. "It is cut and dried."

"Maybe it started that way, brother. And would to The Throne that that were currently true," answered Uriel. "But Raphael is right. There is something else going on even as we speak."

Uriel conveyed very quickly to Michael what he had already made plain to Raphael. Gabriel listened without a word, his hyper-speed brain recording all of the details, being surprised by none of them.

"I see," said Michael, pondering all that he had just heard. "Then even as I fly to access The Throne, the three of you are gonna have to figure out how to deal with all of that. Perhaps we can work it to our advantage, but there is no way forward now without oblation. I'm not sure what mine will be, but we cannot escape it." Michael commed off, leaving his brothers in deep contemplation.

"Raphael…sir?" Raphael heard L'sinell's voice pull him back into what was happening in the Grove.

Almost as one, both tensed and ready for whatever was coming next, Captain L'sinell and Ithokor said, "What are we to do?"

Chapter 9

WE USED TO BE A PLACE
Capitulum Novem

"Do?" said Raphael without moving his head.

"You're all going to make appointments for deep teeth cleaning and dental alignment in my office."

"Dental...*dental* alignment?" said Ithokor.

"Braces, genius," said Tull. "He means we're all getting braces."

"You...you can't be serious," said Ithokor. Ithodor stood without speaking, but he couldn't help the laughs he felt bubbling up inside.

"Do I look like I'm joking?" said Raphael.

L'sinell had seen enough in the last week to understand what Raphael was in truth saying. The "dental appointments" were codespeak for further interrogation and initiation of Covert Ops. The captain had to marvel at how the Twins, seemingly devoid of a functioning brain between them, got under Uriel's charge.

Raphael again raised his head to look at his sword, and finally initiated a big enough sweep to reverse the time stasis over everyone in The Grove. The Throneists and the Dimensioners all came out of it puking and exhausted. Brethren that were now only two dimensional felt their capillaries start to burst but were unable to scream.

"Those of you that can fly and fight and breathe, you will split into two even membered groups. One group will stay here in The Grove and help with cleaning up this mess. There will be personal accountability for each of the foodstuffs that were stolen." Raphael looked around. "The other group will fly with Ithodor and Ithokor to Uriel's mansion to receive whatever instruction Uriel is ready to give. You will answer for your stolen food and destruction of Grove property later. If you need immediate medical attention, or if you need an air mask, my assistants will provide that."

Raphael spoke into his comm to activate his newly created Morgue Unit to begin to collect the brethren that weren't going to survive. His face was stoic, but L'sinell's keen eyes spotted the grief in his heart as he counted up the bodies.

The Leaves used to be the simplest answer to everything, thought Raphael. *But now…now many have been irrevocably tainted. Stained beyond recovery by faith in death.*

"But…but sir…" said one of the still stretching Dimensioners, his voice quavering in and out of flux. "What about us getting home?"

"Uriel will coordinate you. You will get home," answered Raphael.

"Let me supply you all with a piece of knowledge you may not have," interjected Grent. "Before all of this happened, we managed to formerly petition The Throne for the right to stay here. So now we have a legal right to be heard." Grent smiled like someone who had just gained free Bistro rations for a year.

"*You* don't lecture *me* about knowledge, Grent," countered Raphael, his slowly burning anger finally beginning to spill over. "A petition is a request. Not a demand. You don't *have* to be heard."

Raphael's normally smooth brow furrowed as he talked. "You demolished and gorged yourself on food stores that were not yours to consume, in the middle of a classified war zone. You used the most illegal substance in the Realm for wanton property destruction. You set us back weeks, maybe even months, for getting both the food supply and the healing elements back to pre-war normalized levels."

Raphael's gazed locked on to Grent's unbelieving eyes.

"You don't *have* rights."

Raphael suddenly whirled a three-hundred-sixty-degree spin to get a fuller aerial survey of all the recovering brethren.

"This is a bed *you* made that we're all going to have to sleep in, Grent," said Raphael as he hovered over the still stunned onlookers. "Your shortsighted world view has seen to that. So…*all* of you…more succinctly? Shut that mouth and get moving."

Raphael turned his attention to his left, and with a sharp swoop of his wings flew westward to continue his survey.

Ithodor and Ithokor held each other up and began to limp forward. Ithodor couldn't talk, but he used his eyes to tell his brother what he was thinking. Raphael's healers would begin to fly in and assist those who needed it. It seemed for the moment that the fighting had been quelled and orders had been given.

This time both Ithodor and Ithokor knew:

things weren't what they seemed.

CONTINUED IN
Soldiers & Serpents
Tabletop Role Playing Game

**Lucifer: Soldiers, Serpents and Sin – Wings at the Vortex
Interlude 2**
Novella

**Lucifer: Soldiers, Serpents and Sin – Provoke the Past
Book 2**
Novel

FREE RPG Download
Liber RPG downloadium

Soldiers & Serpents

This is a tabletop Role Playing Game where you get to play as some of the characters in the book. It's all about the decisions you make as you fight and go on missions. And every choice you make has intense consequences.

You can download the Beta Version of this game for FREE. Copy and paste this link into your browser: http://bitly.ws/vnMu

If you want to play the full version of the game, you can order that directly.

Write to: dt2author@gmail.com for pricing and shipping info.

ACKNOWLEDGEMENTS
Agnitio

I want to acknowledge the Lord Jesus Christ and His divine love, for showing me on a how to overcome through faith.

I want to acknowledge my late paternal grandmother, Bessie L. Taylor. You are with me in my heart and soul every single day of my life.

I want to acknowledge my late father, David M. Taylor Sr. You were the hardest working man I ever knew. You're still my hero.

I want to acknowledge my author/prophetess/virtuous sister, Wanda D. Gibert. I love you, sis. We're still those two crazy kids running down the hallway in our pajamas eating cinnamon toast.

I want to acknowledge my children, Isuni Taylor and David Taylor III. You two are my heart, now and forever.

I want to acknowledge my friends/staff/support system for being with me for years. Randy, Marsha, Lisa, Melissa. I have not, nor will I ever, forget your kindness and support.

I want to acknowledge my editor for this book, Nicolás Viglietti. Thanks for whipping every page of this book into literary shape.

GLOSSARY
Glossarium

ALPHA CENTAURI – Alpha Centauri is the closest star system to the solar system at 4.37 light-years away. It consists of three stars: the pair Alpha Centauri A and Alpha Centauri B, and a small red dwarf star, Alpha Centauri C, better known as Proxima Centauri, that may be gravitationally bound to the other two.

ANSEL – Grigori Class I, and one of the Grigori commanders in Lucifer's Loyalist army.

ARIEL ARCH WIZDOR – The only female in the entire Realm, she is known for her beauty, her flight speed, her singing voice, and her ability to mesmerize any of the brethren.

ARMORIES – Located both north and south of The City, the armories are storehouses for every kind of weapon that is legally produced in The Realm.

AURORA MOUNTAINS – Snow-capped all year long, these mountains house the Gem Caverns. These mountains also have transparent centers and are different colors depending on what time of year it is. They are full of all manner of cryophilic life.

AZAZEAL – Originally a two-armed, two-winged Class III Grigori, he wanted to gain the respect of his peers. He purposed to fly behind the Wall of Light to directly gaze upon The Throne and ended up getting badly burned, along with all that followed him.

AZAZEALITES – Mutated former Class III Grigori who, due to their attempt to fly behind the Wall of Light, have fused noses and mouths, melted skin, and permanently burnt wings. They can barely breathe, are nearsighted, and their wings are too singed to grant them flight capability.

BASALT – Seraphim Class I, and a captain in Lucifer's Loyalist forces.

BIRTHSILK – The jelly and silk-like substance found inside of Creation Cocoons. It is used to nourish and shape the brethren as they grow and keep them alive until they can emerge from the cocoon.

BLACKFIRE SWORD – Created by the Order of Orali, it is a long sword with a liquid blade made of Throne resin combined with molecules of interstellar space. The blade is encased in clear quartz and has a hand-carved diamond hilt. It is a one-of-a-kind weapon.

B'RELL – Gladiator class, member of Sun Squadron.

BRIMSTONE – Created by Eremiel, it is a rock-like substance that has been combined with sulfur, plasma from the sun, and the glory resin left by The Throne after Gathering. It is highly flammable and was banned from The Realm one year after its creation.

CARMINE – Class I Grigori, larger and stronger than most of his brethren. He is a member of Lucifer's Loyalist army. His favorite weapon is the Laserwhip.

CHERISS – Class III Cherubim, known for their nosy nature, short stature, and chubby frame.

CHERUBIM – Brethren in The Realm characterized by their pink skin, the smell of Refiner's soap, and their four reddish brown wings. They have two eyes in their heads and eyes all over their wings. The Class I Cherubs carry FireSwords and are normally assigned to guard duty of some kind. The Class II Cherubs are foot soldiers or worship leaders. The Class III Cherubs are known as Cheriss and are normally very unaggressive.

CHIRZAH – Grigori Class II, albino, brother to Werx and member of Lucifer's Loyalist army.

COLDFIRE SWORD – An ignitable rapier sword with a thick blue-white blade. It is made from a combination of frost from the Aurora mountains and secret stones from The Garden. Created by the Order of Orali, only twelve swords total were made.

COPPER WARP SPHERES – Globes made up of copper and other metals, with properties that include teleportation, time shifting, explosive capabilities, and disrupting pockets of space and time.

CREATION COCOON – The oblong eggs full of BirthSilk and Creation Jelly where most classes of the brethren are formed. The cocoons are fueled by Genesis Energy, encased in pearl, and as a byproduct of creation, they give off tiny diamonds. They are housed in the Creation Complex.

CREATION COMPLEX – Located in the northeast corner of The City, this is where the Creation Cocoons and Recovery Beds are housed. All the brethren that come into existence from a cocoon are birthed here.

CRYSTAL BOREALIS BOMBS – Explosive devices that can tear a hole in the fabric of reality.

DAGON – Cherubim Class I, and a Subcommander in Lucifer's Loyalist army.

DATA STREAM – A pre-birth information and knowledge feed that instructs the brethren on the basics of life in The Realm. They are fed into Creation Cocoons as each new brother is forming.

DEFLOY – Cherubim Class II, and a member of Lucifer's Loyalist army.

DESTINY WINDOWS – Located in the northwest mountains, these long, stained-glass panels contained the names and the deeds of every brother born into The Realm.

EGAN – Cherubim Class I, and a corporal in Lucifer's Loyalist forces. Assigned to Captain Basalt.

EL-ADRIEL – Junior Gladiator, and friend of Ithodor and Ithokor.

EOS – Pet rat of Lucifer.

EPSILON ERIDANI – Epsilon Eridani is a star in the southern constellation Eridanus, along a declination 9.46° south of the celestial equator.

EREMIEL ARCH WIZDOR – Chief metallurgist, weapons designer, and armor maker for The Realm.

ERIS – One of the seven Kroni, and a Class II Cherubim. Member of Lucifer's Loyalist army.

FACELESS ONE – A member of Michael's Gladiator Elite, and he strongest warriors under Michael.

FIRE MACE – A morning star mace that has plasma cylinders in the handle and can be ignited. Standard weapon of the Seraphim.

FIRE SWORD – Great swords with a double-edged blade made of pure fire, with a red hilt made of a two-handed cruciform, with a pommel. The primary weapon of Class I Cherubim.

FIRST BRETHREN – The very first brethren that were created in The Realm.

FOREVER FORESTS – Located in the extreme southwest region of The Realm, these forests consist of many different types of trees, elements, and stone huts. It is one of the few places in The Realm where names spoken will not turn into whispers.

FROST SHURIKEN – Throwing star weapons with chambers filled with a type of liquid nitrogen. Favored weapon of, and wielded only by, the Zoroasim.

GABRIEL ARCH WIZDOR – One of The Big Three, Gabriel is the multilingual, seven-winged Messenger for all The Realm. He commands his army of Messengers to deliver information as well.

GATHERING – The collective time of worship for all brethren in The Realm, occurring in the Great Hall. Early Gathering is at 6:00 Celestial, and Late Gathering is at 6:00 Primordial.

GEM CAVERNS – Caverns located in the Aurora Mountains. Organic gems are grown in the caverns for every use in The Realm.

GENESIS ENERGY – The energy contained within all Creation Cocoons used to form the brethren growing within.

GLADIATORS – A class of brethren that are the warriors of The Realm, serving under Michael's leadership.

GLADIATOR ELITE – Also known as The Faceless Ones. When they are promoted to the rank of Elite their birth faces are removed and replaced with prosthetic ones. They are the strongest and best warriors of Michael's Gladiator class.

GRENT – Leader of the Dimensioner Army.

GRIGORI – A class of brethren with short stature, white hair, pale blue skin, three arms, and three white wings. Both Class I and Class II Grigori are normally assigned to support other brethren in their duties. Class III became the Azazealites, and there was one Class IV, General Mammon.

HAYYOTH – Creatures that live behind The Veil and have four faces, also known as Tetramorphs. They keep their four faces covered and have four conjoined wings.

HOCK – Grigori Class II, member of Lucifer's Loyalist army.

ICE CHAKRAM – Circular chakram-based throwing weapons with chambers filled with a type of liquid nitrogen. Favored weapon of, and wielded only by, the Zoroasim.

INTHINIEL – Music composer that lived during the time of Orali.

IOAN – One of the seven Kroni, and a Class II Cherubim. Worship Leader protégé of Lucifer.

ITHODOR – Junior Gladiator, formed in the left side of the cocoon with his twin brother, Ithokor. Possesses the ability to sense death.

ITHOKOR – Junior Gladiator, formed on the right side of the cocoon with his twin brother, Ithodor. Possesses Third Sight, the ability to see the auras and energy that surround and inhabit the brethren.

IRIN – One-meter-tall(normally) brethren with square faces set in square heads. They possess beady black eyes, are perpetually hungry, and have flight patterns like slow butterflies, since their wings are perpetually dirty and out of joint. Members of Lucifer's Loyalist army.

KERUBIEL – Class II Cherubim, he was the Worship Leader before Lucifer.

KLE'EM – Grigori Class I, Garrison leader of one of the Grigori phalanxes in Lucifer's Loyalist army.

KREER – One of the seven Kroni, and a Class II Cherubim. Member of Lucifer's Loyalist army.

KRONI – A Cherubim class of brethren that can write their own music and liturgy for worship in Gathering. Lucifer was the first, and there were seven others besides him.

KUVIX – Cherubim Class I, and a corporal in Lucifer's Loyalist forces. Assigned to Captain Basalt.

L'SINELL – Captain in the Throneist army.

LIGHTNING CHARGE – A Gladiator technique invented and perfected by Michael. The Gladiator holds his lightning sword at any chose angle, and spins at his target at hyper-speed.

LIGHTNING SWORD – A broadsword with a blade made of pure lightning. It is the standard weapon of the Gladiator and Gladiator Elite classes.

LOYALIST ARMY – Lucifer's troops that he rallied to his side to create the Rebellion, and usher in the New Order. The army was made up of at least one member of every class of brethren, with some classes numbering into the tens of millions.

LUCIFER – Four-winged anointed Class II Cherubim, owner of the Coat of Many Gems, the first Kroni, Worship Leader, Composer, possessor of an internal Pipe Organ and Tabrets, Light Bearer, the Morningson, Prince of the Grigori, Founder and Leader of the Rebellion.

MAJEL – Class I Grigori, and member of Lucifer's Loyalist army.

MALAKIM – A class of brethren that are known for their diminutive size, being eight centimeters long. They have three fingers and a thumb on each hand, and two pairs of gossamer wings. Unlike most other brethren, they are not formed in a cocoon, but are SpokenBorn.

MAMMON – A four-armed, four-winged, green hued Grigori, the only Class IV in all The Realm. He is one of the generals in Lucifer's Loyalist army. One of Lucifer's first recruits and greatest recruiters.

MEDUSA ELIXIR – An elixir created by Eremiel to help sculpt and solidify works of art made of stone for the StoneWork Circle Gardens. It was later discovered by Lucifer that it could also be used to turn Cherubim into stone, leaving only their tongues as living tissue.

MERCURY PIT – Located north by northwest from The Tower, it consists of a huge circular cavern that overflows with superheated mercury, surrounded by meters and meters of bronze gravel.

MESSENGERS – Gabriel's army of Messenger class brethren that assist him in his information disseminating duties.

MICHAEL ARCH WIZDOR – One of the Chief Princes of the brethren, and one of The Big Three, known for his massive emerald wings and enormous strength. Head of the Gladiator class and Minister of Defense for The Realm.

MILLENNIUM ANCIENT – One of the earliest dispensations of The Throne's rule and establishment of the order of the brethren. It also the first millennium that The Throne began to record the deeds of the brethren.

MILLENNIUM FIRST – The very first thousand-year period that The Throne began to record time.

MILLENNIUM NEW – The current time frame that Lucifer and all the brethren live in.

MINI CITY OF THE ARCH WIZDORS – Located north of The City, the region where the Arch Wizdors live.

NAMELESS ONES – Temporary designation for brethren of any class that have not served long enough to earn a proper name and/or inscription thereof.

NGC 2419 – NGC 2419 is a globular cluster in the constellation Lynx. It is at an approximate distance of 300,000 light years from the solar system and at the same distance from the galactic center.

NODOX – One of the seven Kroni, and a Class II Cherubim. Member of Lucifer's Loyalist army.

OBSIDIAN ORCHESTRA – The orchestra that plays under Lucifer's conducting and composing leadership for Gathering.

OMYN – A mostly silent class of brethren that have a dual existence. Half the time they are stationary stars, and the other half they are comets, moving through interstellar space. They are particularly known for their kaleidoscopic eyes.

OPHANIM – A class of brethren in The Realm shaped in the form of a multi-spoked wheel. Their bodies were made of both wood and flesh, and they had hundreds of eyes on the outer rims of their frame, as well as in the spokes. They have no wings and are mute.

ORDER OF ORALI – A nomadic band of mixed-class brethren who were born in the Mercury Pit. Their skin is scarred from being born in the heat of the Pit. They are metallurgists and weapons makers. They fashioned the twelve ColdFire swords, and the unique BlackFire sword. They briefly studied under Eremiel and then were reassigned to beyond the Far Reaches.

PEREPHAN – One of the seven Kroni, and a Class II Cherubim. Member of Lucifer's Loyalist army.

PROXIMA CENTAURI – Proxima Centauri is a red dwarf star about 4.24 light-years from the Sun, inside the G-cloud, in the constellation of Centaurus.

RÁFOS – One of the seven Kroni, and a Class II Cherubim. Member of Lucifer's Loyalist army.

RAPHAEL ARCH WIZDOR – Chief Healer and leader of the Healer brethren. Raphael is also Keeper of The Leaves.

RAVAGERS – Enormous, crab-like creatures that live in Tartarus and feed off the waste and carrion therein.

SALIX – Gladiator class, Squadron Commander of Sun Squadron.

SANCTUARY – Located 2000 kilometers directly above the far west side of The City, Sanctuary is a secondary place of worship with no limits as to musical structure. All brethren experience Sanctuary worship once per week.

SERAPHIM – A class of brethren characterized by having one red eye & one yellow eye, with six orange-yellow wings that burst into flame when they fly. They all have exceptional speed and strength. Class I are known for their tactical intelligence. Class II, the Guard Seraphs, are known for their organization skill. Class III, the Trihagion Seraphs, have exceptional vocal stamina.

SILK SPINNERS – Nine-legged, spider-like creatures created by The Throne to guard the Oratory, castrate the Zoroasim, and weave any silken royal material needed.

SONIC SWORDS – Hoplite swords that could emit vibrations at various frequencies and bombard its targets with sonic waves as well as cut with its tungsten steel blade. Favored weapon of the Malakim.

SOUND GENERATOR – A distinction for any class of brethren that is capable of producing music internally, without the aid of some external instrument.

STONEWORK CIRCLE GARDENS – Located slightly southeast of The Grove, it is a circular garden that houses various works of art, all made of stone.

SUN SQUADRON COMPLEX – An apartment complex located east of The City in the Outlands. It is where all current members of the Sun Squadron reside.

SUN SQUADRON – A cadre of brethren made up of Gladiators and Junior Gladiators assigned to catalog the daily activities and data readouts of the sun.

TAELUR – Class I Cherubim, one of the main workers assigned to work at the Mercury Pit, a rebellious member of Lucifer's Loyalist Army.

T A R T A R U S – The ultimate garbage dump for The Realm, where all waste products are deposited. The above ground trash dumps, such as the Grey Circle, have their refuse transported into Tartarus at least once per month.

T H E C I T Y – 60,999 square kilometer region where most of the brethren in The Realm live, full of apartment buildings and spires.

T H E C R Y S T A L S E A – Located far north by northwest from The City, it is a large body of liquid comprised of diamonds, oxygen, crystals, water and transparent gold in amorphous states. The Crystal Sea can assume liquid, solid, or gaseous form.

T H E F A R R E A C H E S – Any area of The Realm that is at least as far away as Ursa Major. All star systems in and beyond Ursa Major are counted as a part of the Far Reaches as well.

T H E F O R B I D D E N M O U N T A I N S – Located far north and slightly east of The City, they are a series of mountains that are off limits to every single class of brethren.

T H E G A R D E N – An exclusive, vegetation-based garden located far north and slightly west of The City. It is southwest of the Crystal Sea. It contains plant life and other substances of every type not found anywhere else in The Realm. It is accessed by direct permission from The Throne only.

T H E G R E A T H A L L – Located in The Valley, it is the main place of worship for the brethren, and the space where both Early and Late Gatherings are held.

T H E G R E A T H I L L – A large mound capped by diamonds. It consists of jewels, metals, stone, and wood, covered by enormous amounts of dirt. Brethren are assigned to mine whichever element is available depending on the season.

THE GREY CIRCLE – One of the trash heaps and garbage compacting stations near The City.

THE GROVE – Located 200 kilometers southwest of The Valley, The Grove contains the food supply for The Realm, housing all manner of fruits and vegetables as well as The Leaves. It contains various kinds of other trees and plant life. It also is where Raphael the Healer has his office.

THE HOLY RIVER – Running through the southwest corner of The Realm, it extends far west of The City. Any water drawn from it will purify whatever it touches and burn whatever is evil. It also used to water the organic gems growing in the Gem Caverns.

THE LEAVES – Grown on The Tree of Life, they are golden brown in color. They contain life giving and healing properties and can repair any and all damage done to the brethren in the course of their service to The Throne.

THE MOLE – The Mole

THE NEW ORDER – Lucifer's regime, designed to overthrow The Throne and replace it with himself as the head of The Realm, making him the supreme ruler of every class of brethren.

THE ORATORY – A large, impenetrable building/complex located north of The City where the brethren are required to go no more than once per year to fast, meditate and study. It is also the place where the Zoroasim are castrated, and where all the silk garments for The Realm are made.

THE OUTLANDS – Lands outside of the east City limits. The east Outlands are where the Sun Squadron complex resides, as well as the Sun Door.

THE REALM – The land where The Throne and all the brethren live, centering on The City and reaching out to all the surrounding areas. It encompasses every location above the Sun Door.

THE SUN DOOR – Located due east from The City in the Outlands, the Sun Door is the access point for the sun itself as well as interstellar space.

THE THRONE – The Supreme Power in The Realm, and the Creator and Maker of all existence in all dimensions of life, known and unknown.

THE TOWER – Located in the exact center of The City, The Tower is a spire the stretches above every other building around it. It is a place of information, digital workstations, commerce, mediation, and socialization amongst the brethren.

THE VALLEY – Located far south of The City, known for its blue, yellow and green pastures, it is a massive swath of acreage, filled with ever descending hills. The Great Hall is located here.

THE VEIL – Similar in texture to silk, and magenta in color, The Veil is made of a multithreaded weave of fabric that can't be torn or cut. It covers the Wall of Light during Gathering and absorbs most of its incredible heat.

THE WALL OF LIGHT – A literal wall made of light that covers The Throne in Gathering. It has no ceiling or upper limit. It is made of Throne plasma, joined together by bricks made of solid light and cut into dodecagons and tetrahedrons. Its temperature has been known to reach 5,000,000 Celsius.

TIBENIUS – Grigori Class II, member of Lucifer's Loyalist army.

TREASURIES – The buildings that house all the wealth of The Realm. Their location changes every 24 hours, as the building itself teleports to another location once a day. These locations are known only to The Throne and to the twelve guardians inside each Treasury, a class of brethren known as the Zoroasim.

T R I H A G I O N   S E R A P H I M – Class III Seraphim known for their vocal stamina. They worship before The Throne without ceasing, constantly crying "holy, holy, holy".

T R I S T A N – One of the seven Kroni, and a Class II Cherubim. Member of Lucifer's Loyalist army.

T U L L – Second in command under Captain L'sinell's regiment.

U R I E L   A R C H   W I Z D O R – One of The Big Three, known for his infectious laugh and powerful singing voice, he is the Chief Negotiator and Mediator for The Realm. He is the only one of The Big Three to not command an army.

W E R X – Class I Grigori, brother to Chirzah, and member of Lucifer's Loyalist army.

X A N T H U R – Messenger class, and Lieutenant of Gabriel's Messenger army.

X R O – An Azazealite, and right-hand assistant to Lucifer. He had a harness specially created for him by Lucifer to help him fly.

Z E R M E S – The copper-skinned, black-winged flight trainer for all the brethren, and the last known member of the Dominion class.

Z O R O A S I M – Ebony-skinned eunuchs with metal wings, they are the telepathic guardians of all the Treasuries of The Realm. They use Ice Chakrams and Frost Shuriken in their guard duties, and when they join hands, they can project psionic blasts.

ZOROASIM KATANA – Katana swords whose blades were made of transparent steel that had been folded one hundred times. The hilts were made of polished glass. A weapon wielded only by the Zoroasim.

About the Author

De auctore

David Taylor II is an author, songwriter, producer, educator, playwright, and poet.

He writes sci fi, fantasy, children's literature, and comic books. He is the author of the new children's favorite, *Diary of a Smart Black Kid* and is also adding to his *Dear God* children's series. He is also one of three co-composers for the smash hit theater production, *Eye of the Storm: The Bayard Rustin Musical*, nominated for 3 Black Theater Alliance awards.

The novel, *Lucifer: Soldiers, Serpents and Sin Book 1* is an internationally bestselling Book and has generated an entire story world. The Realm continues to expand, adding coloring books, novels, novellas, RPGs, comic books, and audio books.

He is the writer of the comic series *The Nephilim Wars*, the *Kryo-Karuto*, distributed by Nucleus Comics, and a co-writer in the comic novel *Bloodworld*, distributed by Raincross Press.

He is the proud father of two, as well as a lover of football, pizza, and a good glass of lemonade.